A Shift in Wings

Lost Legacies
Book 5

Maddox Grey

GREYMALKIN

Published by Greymalkin Press
www.greymalkinpress.com

Dev editing by Becca Leigh
Copy editing and proofreading by Ashley Olivier

Cover Design by Seventhstar Art

eBook ISBN: 979-8-9881893-2-9
Paperback ISBN: 979-8-9881893-3-6

The Lost Legacies Series

A Shift in Darkness*

A Shift in Shadows

A Shift in Fate

A Shift in Fortune

A Shift in Ashes

A Shift in Wings

A Shift in Death

A Shift in Tides

*A Shift in Darkness is available for free download at maddoxgreyauthor.com.

Quick Note From The Author

Hey there! I just wanted to chat real quick about what you can expect in this book. This is a fantasy novel that contains adult content and situations. If it was a movie, it would probably be rated "R" for violence, language, and sexual content. If you want to go into this book completely blind and prefer not to read content warnings, you can skip on ahead, my friend.

If there are certain topics that you need to avoid for the sake of your own mental health, or that you simply don't like, please take a look at the list below for some things you will find in this book.

- Reference to depression that leads to suicidal thoughts and actions. The actual event takes place in the past but it is discussed in this book, relevant chapters are 14 & 15.
- Complicated family dynamics, including a parent essentially disowning their child.
- Consensual explicit sex scenes (there is no dub-con or non-con)

- Similar to previous books, this one has lots of fantasy violence and gore.

Also… quick little note on language. I am a strange, strange person, and I've lived a bit of an odd life. I was born and raised in California, but was mostly raised by my Canadian grandmother and was then unofficially adopted by an Irish family in my late teens. You might be wondering why I'm mentioning this, and the reason is that I have a bit of a magpie approach when it comes to the English language.

Sometimes I like the American English spelling… sometimes I'm really attached to that extra "u" and go for the non-American version. Variety is the spice of life y'all.

Bless the soul of my copy-editor because she just sighs heavily at the start of each manuscript and deals with my eccentricities. So if you're an American and looking at a word and thinking it's not spelt right… it is most likely the non-American version of the word.

To all the readers who have supported me on this journey, sent me encouraging messages, and asked for more. Y'all are the absolute best.

And yes, Magos will get his own book, too. Eventually.

Chapter One

"I'm going to enjoy the taste of your blood, valkyrie."

I sneered, "At least you'll get to enjoy something before you die."

My golden wings beat strongly as I hovered in the sky a short distance from the seraph whose brilliant white wings were moving slightly faster than mine because of their smaller size.

He was more agile than me and could maneuver faster in short distances. I could fly longer and in a straight shot would be faster. Thanks to the bloody history between our kinds, we were both well-versed in each other's strengths and weaknesses.

Unfortunately for the seraph, my weaknesses were few, and he was just a scout which meant he wasn't particularly skilled in battle.

And unfortunately for *me*, there was a battalion of very skilled seraphs camped a short distance away, and if I engaged with the scout here, I risked being spotted by them. Great.

"Whenever possible, choose the location of your battle." That was one of the many lessons I'd been working to instill in Bryn, my apprentice, and the young valkyrie had been eager to soak up my words. I'd do well to listen to my own advice now.

Trickery and underhandedness weren't exactly tactics valued amongst the valkyrie. But thanks to being an exile and keeping rather nefarious company these days, my methods had expanded beyond my original training. It had bothered me at first, but I found myself caring less and less about using strategies that many would find unbecoming for a valkyrie.

I let my features shift into a mask of haughty arrogance with the same taunting smile I'd seen on Nemain's face so many times before. "Let's see how fast you can fly on those pitiful wings, vermin."

The seraph's face twisted in rage as he dove for me. But even in this foreign realm, the skies were mine.

My wings beat, fast and true, as I sped away from the scout. I peered over my shoulder to make sure he was following me, instead of doing the smart thing and returning to his unit to report what he had found.

Luckily for me, bloodlust was a common weakness among the seraphim, and this one was no exception. He didn't hesitate as he raced after me. As if one seraph would ever be a match for a valkyrie.

Further and further we flew. Sometimes I'd slow just enough to give him the false impression that he was actually catching up to me before darting away again. Unfettered joy filled me as I sped past, spinning and diving through the air, wind pulling at my hair.

The sun was almost completely down now, and the forests stretching beneath us were already dark and treacherous.

Sigrun, Viggo whined. *I'm bored and hungry. We're far enough away. Quit toying with him.*

Fine, I said reluctantly.

Gunnar enjoyed flying as much as I did, but Viggo found it to be more of a chore. Which to be fair, it was for him. He didn't have wings like us and relied solely on his magic to fly which required a lot of concentration on his part. He also had to maintain a constant state of motion.

Of course, he always had the option to ride on Gunnar's back but he was too stubborn most of the time to take that route.

I added, *Pick a spot to make camp for the night, and I'll catch up to you.*

Alright. Try not to coat yourself in blood this time. There aren't any rivers nearby to wash up in.

I whirled around and hovered in place, waiting for the seraph to catch up. My fingers itched to pull the hammer from my back, but I withdrew the dagger from the sheath on my thigh instead.

"Got tired of running?" the seraph taunted when he finally drew near. "Didn't know the valkyries were such cowards."

I eyed him where his wings kept him suspended in the air, just out of striking range. It was odd to think that the humans had once worshipped such creatures, thinking them to be messengers of some non-existent god. There were plenty of gods that did exist, sure, but none of them associated with the seraphim. But for some reason, the humans thought the seraphim were divine. *Angelic.*

The one in front of me had golden-blond hair and bronze skin. His features were strong and masculine, not handsome, but powerful in a way that pulled you in.

Maybe if he was lounging around playing a harp, I could see why the humans had deemed them beautiful. But the twin fangs that jutted out from a mouth that seemed to be fixed in a permanent sneer made him look more monstrous than anything else. The sharp talons at the end of his fingers were still stained in blood.

The seraphim had delighted in hunting humans before they'd been banished from that realm. And instead of celebrating, the humans had mourned the loss like the foolish species they were.

"Actually," I drawled. "I just wanted to make sure we were far enough away from your friends that they wouldn't be able to rescue you."

"I will tear you to shreds and feast on your flesh," he hissed before his wings snapped, propelling him forward.

I twisted in the air, letting his talons breeze by me while I jammed my dagger into his back, right at the base of his left wing. A pained snarl ripped out of him as he spun, attempting to tear out my throat with his claws. But his wing faltered, making his movement clumsy, and I easily dodged his attack.

"I saw you the other day," I said lightly, eyes narrowing.

He struck at me again, still fixated on my throat, but I ducked my head so that his hit went high and wide over my shoulder.

My dagger struck again, this time opening a jagged gash down his chest. "You grabbed one of the human slaves and pulled them into the sky."

"So what?" He laughed. "Does the valkyrie feel bad for the humans?"

"I don't really give a shit about humans."

Not entirely true. I bore them no ill will and just kind of accepted that they were there. And did idiotic things like worship the monsters that hunted them down.

But not the ones in this realm. They held no false beliefs around the seraphim. I'd been too far away to save the one yesterday, but I could avenge him today.

"But that doesn't mean they deserve to die cruelly."

"They are beneath us," he spat, baring his fangs. "They exist only to serve. Or be a meal."

A flicker of rage broke through my calm battle state, and the hammer on my back instantly seized on it. My grip tightened around my dagger as I drew in a breath to settle the anger.

"Never allow strong emotions to dictate your actions. You cannot deny what you feel, but acknowledge the feelings and then put them aside."

That was a lesson that Bryn handled quite well. Despite her young age, Bryn was always the calm in the storm.

We continued dancing around in the air, the seraph growing sloppier with each attack. He had to be leaking blood from at least a dozen deep cuts, and his wing was close to failing completely.

My playtime was coming to an end. Pity.

This time when the seraph tried to strike at my side, below the ribs, I grabbed his arm and twisted. Hard. He screamed as tendons ripped and bones snapped.

Before he could recover, I struck at his back, severing the tendons completely to one of his wings and wrapping my arms around him like a lover, his back to my chest. His one good arm clung to mine, his talons sinking into my flesh as I kept us both in the air.

"What do you think that human thought when you flew them far above the earth and let them fall?" I whispered into his ear. "Do you think you'll have similar thoughts?"

I shoved him away from me and watched as he futilely tried to beat his wings.

With one so badly damaged, he quickly lost altitude and went into a fast spin. The other wing snapped from the pressure of trying to stop his fall and a howl of agony filled the sky.

Good thing I had led us so far from the seraphim camp, I thought with a smirk.

I dove towards the falling angel, lazily circling around him as his descent continued, only pulling up when he was close to hitting the ground.

Viggo was right. We weren't near any rivers or lakes, and I

didn't want to get caught in the splatter of blood and gore from him hitting the ground.

His scream was cut off with a loud thud, punctuated by multiples bones snapping.

"I hope you find more peace than you ever found in life, human," I offered up the prayer. "And I hope the souls of Hel torment you a little longer, seraph."

It would be days before the scout was missed, and even then, I doubted they would send anyone out to look for him. The seraphim regularly fought with each other. A scout was a low rank. His superior would just assume he'd pissed off the wrong seraph and move on.

I glanced at my arm, seeing the gouges left behind from his talons had already stopped bleeding. Another hour and they'd be gone completely.

I twisted my head around, cracking the joints and releasing a little tension. This side endeavor with the scout wasn't entirely responsible of me since I needed to remain unseen to finish my mission. But when I'd seen him fly off from the campsite, I couldn't resist seizing the opportunity.

A valkyrie could only go so long without a good fight.

And if that fight ended in the death of a mortal enemy? Even better.

———

THE SMOKELESS FIRE crackled and flickered in the night. Not for the first time, I wished Bryn was here. This would have been an excellent training opportunity for her and… I missed the young valkyrie.

It had been a long time since I'd enjoyed the company of another valkyrie and felt that type of kinship. Even though Bryn hadn't been raised among her own kind and hadn't even known she was a valkyrie until recently, her presence was familiar and soothed an old ache in my soul.

But her coming on this mission hadn't been an option. Bryn's grasp on the invisibility spell that we used to hide our wings or our entire bodies was still tenuous, often flickering out in times when she was stressed or distracted. Allowing a small trickle of magic to continually feed the spell would eventually become second nature to her. But she needed more time and a place to practice where the stakes weren't so high.

Plus, with Nemain and so many of the others gone in the dragon realm, Bryn wouldn't have wanted to leave Finn alone no matter how well protected he was in Nemain's apartment.

I stretched my hands towards the flames to warm them up a bit, grimacing at the chill biting at my face from the wind.

The temperature shifts in this realm were rather extreme. The days were blazingly hot, but as soon as the sun set, the nighttime air turned cold and crisp.

The seraphim had fire magic coursing through their veins. Not all of them could wield it, but even then, they tended to burn hot. They probably enjoyed the cooler night temps whereas I only tolerated cold temperatures if there was snow involved, and there wasn't a hint of snow around here.

My eyes flicked into the dark woods surrounding the small clearing, but I still saw no signs of Gunnar or Viggo.

Rationally I knew they'd be fine, but I still worried. If it'd been an option, I would have preferred they stay behind with Bryn and help watch over Finn. But Gunnar would have refused to leave my side, and Viggo would have thrown a fit if I'd taken Gunnar and not him.

So I hadn't even brought it up and just accepted they'd be coming along. It helped having others to take watch anyways so that I could rest.

I reached back and loosened the band holding my braids in a tightly coiled bun and rubbed at my scalp. The golden beads looped around the braids clacked against each other. They weren't entirely practical because of the noise they made, but as long as my hair was tied up, it was fine.

Isabeau and Finn had offered them to me the last time Magos had braided my hair, and I found myself unable to deny them.

When Magos had offered to re-braid my hair months ago, I'd been surprised but grateful because it was in desperate need of attention. While I was aware that many people found my body to be attractive, I wasn't a vain person. My body was merely strong and served me well in battle.

But I had always loved my hair. The black strands were thick and curly, and the feeling of the weight of the braids against my back had always been a source of comfort for me despite how often my mother had complained about them being impractical.

When I'd first been exiled, I'd debated cutting off my hair. I no longer had anyone to help me maintain the braids. But I didn't like being touched by others in general and the mere thought of a stranger touching my hair left me unsettled.

In a rare bout of sheer stubbornness, I'd refused to do so and had just handled braiding my hair on my own. The result wasn't particularly pretty, but it wasn't like I was trying to impress anyone.

Then I'd met Nemain.

The shifter had taken one look at my hair, laughed for a solid ten minutes, and then retrieved Kaysea and Pele to help.

I gazed into the fire, not even really seeing the flames anymore. I was currently coated in dirt and grime after a grueling few days, and I needed to think of something else besides this godsforsaken realm, so I let myself sink into a recent memory.

"You should have come sooner," Magos tutted as my braids slipped through his fingers.

"It's been a busy month." I shrugged even as I enjoyed the feeling of Magos's attention. Our friendship was completely platonic. While I found him very attractive—and it was hard not to considering he was built like a mountain and was a brilliant fighter—it was very clear he was still pining for a lost love.

He wasn't ready for anything else, and I respected that.

"Taking breaks and allowing yourself some reprieve is just as important as physical training," he lectured as he sectioned off my braids and set to the work of unraveling and re-braiding them. Occasionally, he would dip his fingers into a shallow bowl containing a shimmery silver liquid. A gift from Pele.

When I was home, I wrapped my braids up before I slept or sometimes when doing chores. That wasn't always feasible when I was away from home and traveling through some of the more remote realms. One day, when Magos had been fixing my braids, Pele had dropped by claiming she was looking for Nemain. But she'd set a jar full of glimmering oil next to us and said it would help my braids last longer.

It was kind of her. And completely unexpected. I was friends with Nemain, and the shifter was friends with Pele. I rarely interacted with the daemon myself. Our only connection to each other was through Nemain. The luminous substance that smelled slightly of vanilla did exactly as she said. It kept the top of my braids neat for far longer than normal with minimum effort and even if I kept them in longer than I should, my hair never tangled.

I wasn't used to people giving me gifts, and it made me uncomfortable because I didn't know how to repay Pele. When I asked Magos about it, he'd just laughed and said not to question the fact that Pele had accepted me so easily. Apparently, she'd only recently stopped threatening to set him and Mikhail on fire.

"It's strange to be on the other side of a lecture." I smiled.

Magos wasn't nearly as old as me, but he was probably wiser, as I learned a month ago when he was helping me train Bryn. I'd rolled my eyes at him saying he'd picked up some fighting styles in the human realm and he'd promptly put me on my ass with a move he'd learned from a Taekwondo dojo.

He continued working on my hair, shrugging as he said, "One is never too old to learn."

"I'm guessing you repeat that a lot around Nemain?"

He sighed. "At least twice a day."

I chuckled. Despite the sigh, I knew Magos loved being able to teach anyone who would listen.

And Nemain, despite all her complaining, absolutely loved picking up new fighting styles.

When I'd expressed interest in simply entertaining the idea of visiting some martial arts dojos, Nemain had dragged me through a gateway and we'd ended up halfway around the world in a Thailand dojo.

The dojo had been run by the same family for centuries, and they had some sort of history with Magos. It'd been an eye-opening experience, and I had begrudgingly admitted to Magos later that perhaps he was right and the humans did have something to offer.

Although to be fair, not everyone at that dojo was entirely human. Definitely not the family that ran it.

"You should come with us next time we visit," I said. "They say you're long overdue to stop by."

"I would enjoy that." I couldn't see his face, but I could hear the smile in his voice.

A few minutes later, the door burst open and Isabeau raced in. Finn followed in her wake, closing the door behind them and picking up the cloaks she'd knocked off the wall in her haste.

Not for the first time, I thought about how odd it was that Finn was the one prophesied to bring about the end of the realms when Isabeau seemed to fit that role so much better. He was so quiet and thoughtful. And she was an outright terror.

"We brought something for you!" Isabeau announced in a loud voice that was one decimal away from bursting ear drums.

"Inside voice," Magos reminded her.

The young vampire girl rolled her eyes. She was definitely hanging out with Nemain too much. Isabeau gestured towards Finn, but he carefully hung the cloaks back on their hooks before walking over to us; he was never one to be hurried.

"These match your wings," he said, a hint of uncertainty in his voice.

Whereas Isabeau possessed nothing but confidence, Finn was still reserved and unsure about his place with us.

His father was the exiled fae king and very possibly the most powerful fae in existence, but that wouldn't stop me, Nemain, or anyone else in our little group from beating the fuck out of him for how he treated his own godsdamn child.

I peered into the box that Finn held out and saw beads of sparkling gold.

"They're perfect," I said honestly. They'd managed to find the exact same deep gold as my wings. "Thank you both."

Finn placed the box on the table next to Magos, and both the kids watched in delight as he plucked one of the beads out and slid it onto the end of a braid. The rich and vibrant yellow color really did look nice against my black hair.

"You both chose very well," Magos complimented, sliding another bead on.

"Yes, you did," I agreed.

Isabeau beamed, and even Finn's eyes lit up in delight. They watched Magos work for a few more minutes before Isabeau snatched Finn's hand and pulled him towards the door.

"Damon is sleeping, and there is some pineapple pizza in the fridge. I have an idea," she whispered, her voice holding a conspirative edge. But given that Isabeau's idea of whispering was basically speaking at full volume, it wasn't really much of a secret.

"If you make a mess, you clean it up," Magos said calmly.

Isabeau just looked at him with innocent wide eyes before turning back to Finn. They stood there for a few minutes merely staring at each other before Isabeau continued tugging him out of the apartment.

"So, they still talk to each other telepathically then?" A worried frown pulled at the corners of my mouth.

"Yes." Magos reached over and snagged a bead out of the box. "Neither Jinx nor Eddie can overhear them unless Isabeau allows it, and she's still able to walk into all of our minds without us having the faintest idea she's in there."

"Fuck," I muttered.

"Pretty much," Magos agreed.

None of us had the faintest clue how or why Isabeau held this ability, but she was still years away from puberty. If she was already this powerful, what the hell would she be capable of when she fully came into her power?

The conversation had turned to lighter topics when Mikhail walked in and froze at the sight of Magos re-braiding my hair.

Mikhail was the opposite of Magos in many ways. Most days, arrogance practically dripped off him and like Nemain, he had a sharp tongue and was quick to violence. I still wasn't entirely sure whether him and Nemain were going to kill each other or fuck each other. Both seemed likely.

But that day, there wasn't a trace of arrogance on Mikhail's beautiful face. Instead, he looked mournful, as if he glimpsed the ghost of a loved one. Without a word, he spun on his heel and walked out.

Magos paused, and I twisted around to look up at him, a question in my eyes.

"Mikhail doesn't like to think about our home realm, Cerulle, and what life was like there." Magos gave me a sad smile. "He's buried almost every aspect of our culture. Even changed his name." He shrugged.

I knew that Mikhail used to be able to summon a sword the way Magos could, but he no longer had the ability. When I'd asked Nemain about it, she'd gotten an odd, pained look on her face and had refused to talk further about it.

"Braiding hair was an important part of our culture," Magos explained as he continued to braid the section he held in his hands. "Mikhail likely remembers watching his parents braid each other's hair while he was growing up. He's been very careful not to comment on the fact that I'm growing my hair out again, after keeping it shorn for centuries."

"We can do this at my place," I offered, frowning in thought at his words. At the pain behind them.

Mikhail wasn't the only one who had a complicated history with his past and culture. I didn't want to make things harder for him even if I did find him to be an arrogant ass most of the time.

"Thank you." Magos paused for a moment before resuming his work. "But it's time my nephew stopped avoiding our history. However agonizing it may be."

Abruptly, I stopped reminiscing as the hair on the back of my neck stood on end. I was no longer alone.

With a casual ease, I leaned back, forcing my body to remain relaxed while my eyes scoured the forest. A branch creaked from somewhere above me, and my gaze shot upward just in time to see a dark shape take to the sky.

I launched myself through the tight space between the trees until I was hovering above them, spinning in a slow circle with a dagger in hand.

Nothing.

But there had been something. Something with wings.

But the seraphim had white wings that were easy to spot, day or night.

This definitely hadn't been a seraph.

I continued to scour the night skies, but there was nothing out of place. I wasn't that familiar with all the wildlife in this realm; maybe it was nothing.

Sigrun? Viggo called from below. *We brought food.*

After one final look around, I flew back down to our camp to have some dinner. It'd been a long day, after several long weeks. I told myself I was getting tired and a little paranoid.

But no matter how much I repeated that to myself, I still couldn't shake the feeling I was being watched.

Chapter Two

I'm bored and sick of looking at these winged assholes.

Gunnar's piercing blue eyes glared at the much smaller cat who'd been complaining nonstop for the past hour.

The skogkatt was crouched next to him so when the wolf snapped open his solid white wings, he sent Viggo flying. Viggo snarled from where he landed unharmed on the forest floor and he crouched down, muscles tensing as he readied himself to leap onto the white wolf.

Knock it off, I ordered. Even telepathically, there was a bite to my tone.

Gunnar tucked his wings in close and pointedly ignored the skogkatt, who was still staring daggers at him. They'd been like this all day, and it was wearing on my last nerve.

My eyes quickly scanned the hundreds of seraphim camped in the valley beneath us, making sure none of them had heard the commotion. The tension eased from my muscles as they continued to settle into their temporary camp, tearing chunks of meat off the carcasses that hung draped over the fire pits scattered around the campsite.

We'd been in the seraphim realm for over a week now,

scouting various cities and collecting information while staying out of sight. Aside from taking out that seraph scout a couple days ago, we'd been in pure reconnaissance mode, and the lack of action was wearing on all of us.

I was a *valkyrie*. Not a godsdamned spy.

But Viggo and I both had the ability to turn ourselves invisible, and I could extend my spell to hide Gunnar from sight as well, which made us uniquely suited for this mission.

At least, that had been Pele's opening argument for why she wanted us to stay behind after we helped Nemain steal some dragon fangs from a seraph general. I'd looked at her like she was crazy and refused to entertain the idea of remaining in the seraphim realm while my friends went off to consort with dragons.

Given that I could fly, it'd made far more sense for me to be part of that crew instead of skulking about on an information-gathering mission.

But while Pele was many things, crazy wasn't one of them. Ever since the dark seidr practitioner Gullveig had laid a rather elaborate trap near my home that had put Bryn in her crosshairs, I had been determined to track down the bitch and end her once and for all.

Unfortunately, locating an evil sorceress who had convinced the world she was dead and been hiding for centuries wasn't exactly easy.

I'd made little progress, and while Nemain had offered to help, she had more than enough on her plate between dealing with fae bullshit, helping Eddie, and trying to stay one step ahead of the warlocks and vampires. I refused to add yet another problem to her long list of problems.

And that's where Pele stepped in, smooth as the fucking devil.

Daemons are ruthless when it comes to collecting information, none more so than Pele. She could be arrogant and a little too brazen for my taste, but when she promised to track down Gullveig for me, I believed her.

Truth be told, I hadn't been expecting to find much here. But I was glad I'd accepted Pele's offer. Not only because it would hopefully lead me to Gullveig, but because Pele was right. There really was something going on here.

My wings shifted, causing the leather satchel on my back to rub against them. I was running out of paper, but Pele would be happy with the maps and population information I'd gathered so far.

The seraphim were clearly preparing for battle. All of their cities had been reinforced to withstand sieges, and they were conducting regular training exercises.

That hadn't been all that surprising. We suspected that they were working with the exiled fae king, and nobody would use the seraphim for anything other than soldiers. Just point them in a direction and they would be happy to slaughter everything in their path.

What I had not been expecting was the presence of humans.

It had been the same in every city we'd been to thus far. Each one had a small area where humans were kept. In pens. Like cattle.

Given the discarded human bones we'd found, it was clear the seraphim hadn't lost their taste for mortal flesh.

But we'd been through well over a dozen cities at this point, and there were hundreds more. Assuming they all had humans in them, there had to be well over a hundred thousand humans in this realm. I didn't know much about the human realm, but I doubted the seraphim had snatched them from there.

Aside from the fact that someone would have noticed if a hundred thousand mortals vanished without a trace, the seraphim were forbidden from entering that realm. They physically couldn't enter thanks to the protective spell cast by the fae and daemons.

So where the hell did they get these humans from?

I'd tried speaking to a few of them, but my translation mark failed to understand their language.

Based on the confused and fearful expressions on their faces when I'd tried to reassure them I meant no harm, they didn't understand me either. They merely stared at my wings in horror as they crowded protectively around each other. Not that I took offense; I *could* be quite terrifying.

My wings were gold, not white like the seraphim, but that didn't matter to them. To mortals, anything with wings represented death. I'd stopped approaching them in cities because my presence only served to frighten them, and they couldn't communicate with me anyway.

But the way these humans looked at me struck a chord deep within my soul. They didn't know what I was and just assumed I was some type of seraphim, but the mistrust and terror I glimpsed in their eyes was the same I saw in the eyes of other valkyries. Once upon a time, I had been one of the most respected and revered amongst my kind. I had been one of the strongest valkyries in existence even before I had bonded with *him*.

Now there was no question I was the most powerful valkyrie. But the price I paid for my gifts left me an exile. The power itself was never something I desired.

I'd only wanted to save my friend from himself, and I had assumed my death would be the price. It hadn't worked out that way.

I didn't regret the choices I made. But the toll of carrying them grew a little heavier every time a valkyrie looked at me with fear and revulsion.

Are we going to follow this group or continue on to the next city?

Viggo asked as he moved to settle down in front of me, cocking his head.

I thought about it as I absently stroked his fluffy coat. We'd seen several large battalions like this over the past few days, all heading south.

Let's follow them, I decided. *We haven't learned anything new in the last few cities; they all have the same basic layout. Maybe we'll learn something new if we follow this group to their destination.*

And then we can go home? Viggo said hopefully.

My lips pressed together in a flat line. *You know we can't. Not yet.*

He rolled onto his back, stretching out his legs while offering me his belly. I dutifully gave him pets. *Where will be go then?* he inquired as a deep purr rumbled out of him.

Emerald Bay. We need backup, I admitted, albeit with a smidge of reluctance. *Pele might not have returned yet from the dragon realm, but Asmodeus could have information for us. The wards around Nemain's place are strong enough to give even Gullveig pause, so we can rest there while we figure out our next move.*

The purring stopped as Viggo glared at me. *You can't expect me to stay there. With that fae asshole.*

I'm pretty sure you're the one who started shit with Jinx, I pointed out with a snort.

Viggo twisted and sprang to his feet. *I'm getting something to eat.* He stalked off towards the sparse forest behind us.

I glanced at Gunnar, and he let out a long-suffering sigh before trailing after the sulky feline. The Niflheim wolf couldn't speak like Viggo, but after five centuries of companionship, we understood each other just fine.

Despite their constant bickering, Gunnar felt very protective of Viggo. He was the one who'd found the skogkatt cub alone in the woods, wounded and alone. Much the same way I'd come across Gunnar centuries before.

A small smile played across my lips as I watched them head

deeper into the woods before I turned my attention back to the seraphim camp.

Prickles ran up the back of my neck, and I shifted my gaze towards the woods behind me.

Ever since that night I'd seen something in the trees, I hadn't been able to shake the feeling that we were being followed. I was reasonably confident that it wasn't a seraph, as they had little patience and would have attacked me by now. But I had no doubt that Gullveig would be interested in having me followed, and she was definitely capable of finding someone who was good at remaining unseen and patient.

I exhaled a frustrated breath and focused on the seraphim again as I pondered what to do about our stalker. Maybe once the seraphim settled down for the night, I could go on a little hunt of my own.

———

AFTER LOCATING a small clearing a safe distance away from the camp, I gathered up some firewood and set about stacking it into a neat pile. With one whispered word, flames burst to life and danced across the branches. Not a hint of smoke to be seen.

The fire also gave off no scent, which made me a little sad because I loved the smell of a campfire. But my practical side almost always won out over my whimsical one.

Okay, I didn't really have a whimsical side. I had practical and slightly less practical.

Viggo and Gunnar should be back soon. Once we finished eating, I'd telepathically tell Viggo to do a sweep and see if he could track down our mysterious friend while Gunnar and I played bait.

It hadn't worked the past few nights, but there was always the chance that whoever was watching us would slip up and

Viggo would find them. If that didn't work, then I'd go for a walk through the woods and see if that would tempt them out. Neither Viggo nor Gunnar would like that plan, but I'd deal with that argument later.

Reaching into my bag, I pulled out a piece of charcoal and the map I'd been working on.

I sketched in the river that we crossed earlier this morning, along with extending the forest I'd started to draw yesterday and the mountain range ahead of us.

An awareness prickled at the back of my mind even as my fingers continued their work.

Hello, stalker.

Twisting to the side, I pretended to be looking for something in the leather bag while I set the map down out of harm's way. It would be really annoying to get blood on it after spending so much time plotting everything out.

I rose to my feet and took a few steps away from the tree I'd been resting under. Flexing my fingers at my sides, I refrained from instinctively pulling out a dagger or calling my hammer. I wanted to have a chat with whoever was following me before I tore them apart.

"I know you're there." My eyes rose to the thick branches of the tree where my instincts told me something was wrong.

There was nothing about the feeling I could articulate or explain, but I knew with one hundred percent certainty that someone lurked in the shadows.

After a few seconds, some leaves shook from a branch midway up the tree, and a hooded figure dropped to the ground. Their landing was smooth but still jarring enough to cause their hood to slip back.

Huh. Not exactly what I was expecting. My stalker didn't look like any species I knew of from the Yggdrasil realms…

In fact, he almost looked fae.

The dark-haired stranger rose to his full height. At just over six feet, I was hardly short, but he had at least a couple inches on me.

In less than a second, I took in and catalogued every detail relevant to a fight. Broad shoulders and a strong, lean build. Just enough bulk that a punch from him would hurt, but not too bulky that he'd be slow. He held a sword in one hand and a short, curvy dagger in the other.

Fuck. I hated sword fighters. My fighting style relied on strength and overpowering my opponents. Which usually wasn't hard because few fighters could match my skills. I sparred with Nemain and her vampire groupies every chance I had because it was hard to find better sword fighters than those three. I could hold my own against them, but not without ending up cut to shit.

If he was any good, and I very much suspected he was, then I was going to bleed a lot in this fight. Annoying. But I'd heal as soon as I put him down.

Surprise flickered through me when I took in the stranger's face. Something about his features screamed fae to me… but not sidhe. His features were too rough and masculine for the sidhe, who leaned towards androgyny.

Who the fuck was this guy, and why was he following me?

"Fancy wings." Blue eyes the color of a sunny, cloudless day flicked curiously over my golden feathers. "What are you?" He tilted his head.

"Pretty sure my gold wings are a big fucking clue," I replied smoothly even though I was a little thrown off by his question.

He had to know what I was if he'd been sent by Gullveig, and I wasn't kidding about the wings being a clue. Valkyries were the only species to have golden feathers, and we were well-known across all the realms. Unless…

I scrutinized him further and took a shot in the dark.

"If you don't know what a valkyrie is, then I'm guessing you've been hiding away in some godsforsaken realm. You're one of those devourer fae freaks, aren't you?" I couldn't see magic, not without casting a spell, but I could feel it. And his magic felt *wrong*.

It was the same wrongness that I felt off Finn and Nemain when they used their magic. I'd mostly gotten used to it from them, but coming from a stranger it made me wary.

"Valkyrie," he said slowly, as if tasting the word on his tongue. His eyes narrowed as he processed the rest of what I'd said. "Freak seems a bit rude. Especially since I come bearing gifts."

I made a show of giving him a thorough once-over. "Funny. I don't *see* any gifts."

"Again with the rudeness," he muttered even as a grin twitched across his lips. "I've been in this realm for a few weeks, and I overheard these winged pricks talking about a group of misfits who showed up here recently, practically decimated a city, and then left through a gateway."

The alarm bells that had started going off when I suspected he was one of the devourer fae hybrids began blaring even louder. Gullveig sending someone to spy on me here would have been annoying but expected. Pele had suspected the seraphim were working with Balor, most likely through Lir, but I'd yet to see any of his warriors in this realm.

But one of them had clearly found me and knew that Nemain had been up to something here. I wasn't sure why he was following me or why he had come alone, but once I figured that out, I'd take care of him and get the hell out of this realm.

"Nothing to add?" he asked when I remained silent. He shrugged. "It's fine. You don't have to say anything. It was a feline shifter who opened the gateway. I only know of two feline shifters with that type of magic, and from my brief interaction with them, I'm confident that they're both insane and brazen enough to antagonize an entire city of psychopathic warriors who can rain down fire."

"Watch how you speak about my friends," I warned. Not that I really considered Badb a friend; I barely knew her, but he didn't need to know that.

"Are you really going to stand there and tell me neither Nemain nor her mother are at least a little psychotic?" He raised a dark eyebrow with a scoff.

Nemain absolutely was a little insane. She was also short-tempered and had questionable morals. Based on my brief interactions with Badb, I was pretty confident this was a case of the apple not falling far from the tree. But despite her questionable sanity, when Nemain gave someone her loyalty, she would go through hell for them.

And I was one of the few people who could claim that type of loyalty from her. In many ways, I thought of Nemain as a younger sister.

Which meant I could talk shit about her, but *nobody* else could.

"The only thing that matters is that I claim her as a friend." I took a step forward, and he eyed me warily but held his ground. "I don't know you. Which makes you an enemy until you prove otherwise."

The fae warrior continued to point his sword in my direction, the blade shining beneath the moonlight. His arm never faltered as he held the blade perfectly perpendicular to the ground.

Curiosity piqued inside me. The fae mostly relied on their magic, and some also trained as warriors, but I'd never encountered any that were all that good. Whoever my stalker was, he had training and experience. Nemain had told me about Balor and his army, but I hadn't encountered any of them yet.

Nemain said they not only possessed strong magic abilities but were also skilled fighters. I wanted to know just how skilled they really were.

"Something tells me you don't have many friends, which means you move through life thinking everyone is a potential enemy." His voice was smooth and deep with a lilting accent that I sometimes heard from the older fae, although his was much more pronounced. It was pretty, but that didn't detract from the truth of his words.

"Your point?" I retorted, schooling my features into nothing but disinterest, even as I inwardly flinched. I could count the number of friends I had on both hands, which considering my age was more than a little pathetic.

His expression turned thoughtful. "Just seems exhausting is all."

"And what? You go through life assuming everyone is your friend?" I scoffed. "Seems foolish."

And why the hell was I having this conversation with him? I should be grabbing my hammer and smashing his head in. It was that damn accent that was more than a little soothing.

He gave me a placating smile like I was a child who had said something amusing. "I've lived a long time. Maybe you'll change your outlook as you get older."

The curiosity I'd been feeling about his fighting abilities and accent snapped into white hot anger at the patronizing words. The fae and their godsdamn *arrogance*.

Magic sparked from the hammer, and it shot into my outstretched hand from where it had been resting beside the tree. For the first time since our interaction started, uncertainty flashed in his eyes as his stare lingered on the weapon.

"When you've lived as long as *I* have," I said, raising the hammer slightly, "you learn to expect the worst from people. They rarely disappoint."

He started to lower his sword. "Wait—"

I didn't.

I lunged forward and swung at his head. He ducked beneath my blow and slashed with his dagger at my side.

But I didn't try to dodge. As the blade sunk into my flesh, I slammed my elbow down onto his outstretched arm. He let out a pained grunt as tendons tore and bones crunched. My other arm was already swinging, and he flew backwards when my hammer crashed into his abdomen and a spark of its magic burst free.

I growled at the hammer as I yanked it back. I'd only meant to physically hit him, not use its magic. It was getting harder and harder to deny the hammer's true nature.

I looked away from it just in time to see the fae twist in midair so that his feet hit the thick trunk. For a split second, he was crouched perfectly horizontal to the ground before he pushed off and landed a few feet in front of me.

He'd lost his dagger, but he still had his sword. My eyebrows shot up as he flashed me a happy grin.

A direct hit like that should have crushed his chest.

Even with the healing magic that all fae possessed, he should have been down for at least a few minutes while his body pieced the broken bones and smooshed organs back together. What the hell…

"Nice hit. I was wondering just how strong you were."

"So you decided to find out by letting me hit you?" I asked incredulously. "Who the fuck are *you?*"

"Name's Niall." As soon as the name left his mouth, he moved almost faster than I could track.

My shield sprang out from the gold bracer I wore on my right arm, colliding with his sword with a deafening clang that hurt my ears.

His head cocked to the side as he took in my shield. "Nice. Where can I get me one of those?"

The fae whirled around, fighting with a tenacity he lacked before. As I used my shield and hammer to block his strikes, I realized he'd been holding back when we first dueled. He was just as fast as Nemain and almost as strong as me. But thus far, he had yet to use any magic.

Either he didn't possess any offensive magic, or he was holding back for some reason. Maybe whatever he had was too slow for a fight like this.

Good for me. Bad for him.

"Or even better"—he caught my hammer against his sword when I swung for his head and peered at it admiringly—"where can I get a hammer like yours?"

I growled and called forth my shield before slamming it into his side. He stumbled back, laughter pouring out of him.

"Touchy about the hammer, are we?"

I closed the distance between us as I went on the offensive.

But not only did he match me blow for blow, but more than a few of his strikes also made it past my guard. I was bleeding from at least a dozen cuts, some of them deep enough to be problematic.

Not enough to kill me, but I could already feel myself slowing down from blood loss.

And that wasn't my only problem.

Magic thrummed from the hammer, skittering across my skin like little lighting strikes. Its power had been calling to me more and more lately, and it had enjoyed being wielded seconds ago. But now it wanted another taste of my opponent.

"There are no hammers like mine," I snarled, leaping for him and dropping the hammer a split second before I crashed into him and pulled my dagger free.

Blood trickled down his neck from where my blade bit into his skin, but I felt the same bite at my throat.

Shit.

Keeping his head perfectly still, his gaze fell to where the hammer lay a few feet away before he met my eyes once again. "Why drop the hammer for the dagger?"

Because my resolve against using its magic is weakening, and I'm just angry enough to say fuck it and fry your fae ass.

"I want to feel your blood flow over my hand before I smash your body apart," I said instead.

"Liar." He narrowed his eyes at me. "A slit throat will barely slow me down. And I suspect the same is true for you. What's so special about that weapon?"

The fae's bright blue eyes bore into me, and his features morphed until they resembled that of another. One with a strong jaw line, a slightly crooked nose, and a scar beneath his left eye.

Fight, flight, or fuck, a deep voice full of amusement rumbled through my mind.

We'd never done the latter, as that had never been our relationship. We'd done plenty of the first two throughout our centuries of friendship and partnership.

I blinked and the image was gone, leaving only the fae male standing before me and a hollow feeling in my soul. Both of us were breathing heavily, inches apart, with our blades still angled at the other's necks.

He was right, a slit throat wouldn't kill me. It wouldn't even slow me down, not for a few minutes anyway.

The magic from the hammer was still calling to me, burning through my veins, making me ache for another round of fighting. Or a solid fuck.

It would absolutely not be the latter, so I went with the fighting option. I shoved away from him, ignoring the burning slice across my neck. The trees were too dense for me to fly and use air attacks, but I had enough space for something else. I hurled myself even further back to increase the distance between us, then I shot up into the air and pulled my wings tight, spinning rapidly. They shot open, sending several hard-pointed feathers outward.

The fae warrior tried to lunge to the side, but I'd spread them in a wide enough arc that he couldn't dodge all of them.

A snarl ripped out of him as my spear-like feathers pierced the left side of his body. I was on him before he could recover, sweeping his feet out from under him and straddling his hips. The jagged feathers of my wings were aimed at his face while my dagger rested beneath his chin.

"Who. Are. You?" I demanded.

"I already told you." He bared his bloody teeth at me in a feral smile. "I'm Niall."

"Give me one reason to not splatter your blood across the forest floor, *Niall*." I put a little more pressure on the dagger, forcing him to tilt his head back further.

His eyes darkened for a moment. "Your friend… the shifter with the smart mouth," he said slowly. "She spared my life. Maybe you should check with her."

I laughed, and he grimaced against my blade. "Nemain doesn't spare anyone. She lives and breathes violence. If the two of you crossed paths, you'd be dead."

He muttered something under his breath that I was pretty sure I misheard, so I nudged him with the dagger.

"Speak up," I hissed.

"You were right earlier," he admitted. "I am one of Balor's creations, a fae tainted with devourer magic. A while back, I was with a group who attacked Nemain in one of the fae realms. She killed the others and got the better of me in a fight. But she spared my life."

"Bullshit." I didn't bother to hide the disbelief from my voice. Nemain was a lot of things, but soft-hearted wasn't one of them. She would slit someone's throat in the middle of a meal and go back to eating next to their cooling corpse.

She'd also never mentioned choosing to leave one of her enemies alive.

Something flickered across his face. Regret? Desperation? I didn't know him well enough to tell.

"Not bullshit. Ask her and she'll tell you." That cocky grin graced his mouth again. "I'm sure she'll remember me."

We stared at each other, my thighs resting on either side of his hips. I kept my expression even despite the hesitancy I was feeling. If Nemain really had spared him, she must have had a reason.

He shifted slightly, and my wings surged forward until the points were less than an inch from his face.

"Sorry, just trying to adjust… things." He let go of his sword and slowly rotated his hands until both palms were facing up. "It's been… awhile… since I've had someone so beautiful on top."

I froze, at a complete loss for words, as I realized exactly where I was positioned over him. It'd been a while for me, too. Once upon a time, there was nothing I enjoyed more than a fuck after a good fight. Even better if the person I was fucking was the one I'd been fighting.

But sex required a level of trust I didn't have with most people these days. And despite how physically attractive this fae warrior was, I sure as shit didn't trust him.

Those sharp blue eyes looked at me, and I got the distinct impression that he understood everything that had just passed through my mind and felt the same. It was strange, as I knew nothing about him, but I suddenly felt this odd kinship.

Sigrun? Viggo asked tentatively.

I didn't take my eyes off Niall, but I sensed the skoggkat somewhere behind me, likely still cloaked in his invisibility because Niall gave no reaction to him joining us in the clearing.

"Everything's fine," I said out loud for Niall's sake. "It appears we'll be having a guest joining us for dinner."

Chapter Three

NIALL STROLLED over to the campfire and sat cross-legged in front of it. He tilted his head as he looked at the flames curiously. "The smokeless fire is a neat trick."

I grunted in response and retrieved the rabbit-like creature Gunnar had brought back.

It only took me a few minutes to skin it and cut away some chunks to cook over the fire. Viggo and Gunnar had already eaten, but I tossed them the remains anyway. Wordlessly, I handed over some lightly seasoned meat on a stick to Niall and took a seat opposite him.

"Talk," I ordered as I held my portion of the meat over the flames. "You have until I finish eating this meal to convince me not to kill you and leave your body here to rot."

He chuckled. "Well, I appreciate you providing me with one last meal and the pleasure of your company if that's the case." He smiled broadly at me.

I glared at him over the fire.

"Your eyes have a red sheen." He squinted at the fire and back at me. "They didn't before, but with the light of the fire, they do. Is that a valkyrie thing?"

Niall's cavalier attitude towards me and the situation was really beginning to throw me off.

Less than an hour ago, we'd held blades at each other's throats. And I'd literally threatened to kill him just moments ago. But he was acting like we were simply old friends catching up over a campfire.

This had to be some type of game to get me to lower my defenses.

"Yes," I said almost hesitantly, "it's a valkyrie thing."

It's not like it was some secret. Everyone knew that valkyries had golden wings and that our eyes took on a red sheen in firelight.

Niall was either an excellent liar, or he really had no idea what valkyries were. Which was just odd. We may not meddle in the affairs of others like the fae and daemons, but we were well-known across all the realms.

"Hmm," he hummed thoughtfully as the flames dancing between us captured his attention again. "The fire might not cast off any smoke or scent, but it's still visible. If a seraph were to fly overhead, they'd spot it easily."

"They rarely fly at night; their night vision sucks." I turned my meat so that it cooked evenly. "Besides, if they were to find us right now, that'd be a problem for you, not me."

With half a thought, I activated my invisibility spell and blinked out of existence. Viggo did the same, and I extended my spell to include Gunnar as well, leaving Niall sitting all alone.

He sat up straighter as he looked around, trying to spot us. Shoving the stick into the ground so that his meat continued to cook, he rolled to his feet and walked around to where I was still sitting. My lips twitched with amusement as Niall dropped to his knees and studied the area where he'd seen me sitting seconds ago before stretching out his hand and poking me in the shoulder.

"I can't see your magic." His brows furrowed together. "I can see the trace of magic over the fire, but I can't see the magic you just used to hide yourself from sight."

"You sound surprised." I released the magic with a soft sigh. I'd been using it a lot the last week, and it was beginning to wear on me.

"I'm fae." He shrugged a shoulder and gave me a crooked grin that made my heart beat a little faster. "I've never encountered magic I couldn't see before. Sometimes I don't understand what I'm looking at, but I can always see it. Just when I thought there was nothing new left to see, you give me this gift."

"I thought you were supposed to be the one giving me a gift." I arched an eyebrow at him and then looked at where his hand was now resting on my shoulder.

"And I will." He let his hand linger for a few more seconds before removing it and taking a seat next to me instead of returning to the other side of the fire. "Knowledge is what I have to offer, and I promise to not withhold anything, but I can't help but be curious about you and your magic. How does the spell work? Can all valkyries cast it?"

"I'm not here to sate your curiosity." I pulled my stick away from the fire to let the meat cool and gave him a look full of warning. "Tell me why you are here and why you tracked me down."

"Question for a question?" he offered as he removed his roasting food from its spot beside the fire.

"This isn't a negotiation," I growled.

"Neither of us are going anywhere tonight." His gaze slid to the hammer that was resting on the ground in front of me. "What harm is there in having a civil conversation?"

"I don't know much about you," I said coldly. "The little I do know is that you work for Balor, you tracked me down in this realm, and you've shown an awful lot of interest in my hammer, which tells me that you know more about me than you're letting on."

Gunnar punctuated my words with a deep growl from where he was laying like a sphinx a few feet away from Niall. If looks could kill, Viggo would have already rendered the fae deceased.

This was usually the part where someone would stammer and quickly try to explain themselves. But Niall just smiled and took a bite of his meat.

"This is good," he mumbled as he tore off another chunk. "I was expecting it to be sweeter, but it's got a richer flavor than that. The spices you added are perfect." When I continued to glare at him, he gestured to my stick. "You should eat before it gets cold."

"There's something wrong with you," I grumbled and then took a bite.

Damn it. He wasn't wrong. This was pretty tasty. Not nearly as gamey as the previous meals had been. I'd have to ask Gunnar to hunt down more of these for our remainder of time in this realm.

We ate in companionable silence for a few minutes. Once we were both done, I carved up the second rabbit-like creature, and we both held our sticks over the fire again. I had to admit that this was kind of nice even if I was still debating killing him once I got the information I needed.

I mused it over while the flames danced in the night. Niall clearly didn't know anything about Valkyries, but it's not like our abilities were a secret.

I had some advantage over him while he remained in the dark about them, but I also wanted information from him. Something told me he'd be hard to beat it out of, so playing along meant me getting what I wanted that much faster.

"It's a basic Vanir illusion spell," I said, answering his question from before. "Almost everyone from the Yggdrasil realms can cast it. It's not that effective in the Yggrasil realms because almost everyone there can also see through the spell. But outside of those realms, it's quite effective."

Niall quirked an eyebrow, rotating his meat over the flames. "Yggdrasil?"

My eyes roamed over him as I pondered how to answer. He sat only a couple feet away from me, casually reclined on one hand with his long legs stretched out towards the fire. His friendliness and casualness was really throwing me off because it was decidedly un-faelike. On top of that, he didn't seem the least concerned about any hostility I aimed at him.

"Yggdrasil is how we refer to the eight realms that are connected. Nine if you count the human realm but we don't really consider that one of ours," I explained. "Like the fae realms, the Yggdrasil ones have thinner walls separating them. There are plenty of natural gateways between all of them."

"I've never heard of them, but they sound interesting. Maybe I'll get to see them someday," he said wistfully.

I eyed him with attentive curiosity. Everyone knew of the Yggdrasil realms. The events of Ragnarok had primarily played out in the human realm, and the fallout had impacted many.

While my people had largely retreated into the other eight realms, we still interacted regularly with the fae and daemons.

Balor and the bulk of his army might still be locked away, but we knew he'd managed to get many of his followers out, like Lir, and they had ways of communicating back to him. Apparently, any information that was sent back about what was going on outside their realm of exile wasn't shared with the bulk of his army.

I wasn't exactly sure how that information was useful, but I'd let Pele know regardless. Whatever helped and all.

"That was two questions, so you owe me two answers."

I stared into the flames as I thought about what to ask him.

Niall might not act like any fae I'd encountered before, but that didn't mean he didn't have their level of craftiness when it came to speaking the "truth".

The fae did their best not to lie, because magic was so intrinsic to who they were that sometimes it would do odd things with the words they spoke. If a fae wasn't careful, they could find themselves bound by the truths or lies they uttered.

Simple questions were my best bet.

"How long have you been locked away with the exiled fae king?"

Niall glanced at me. "Since the beginning."

For a split second, I completely froze. I quickly covered up my shock by pulling my meat away from the fire and examining it before putting it back to cook a little longer.

According to Nemain, Balor and his army had been locked away since 2500BC. Niall looked to be in his late thirties. The fae lived a long time, but they didn't live forever, and they did visibly age. Just slowly over a thousand years, maybe two thousand if they had particularly strong magic.

I'd assumed that Niall was the child of some fae who had been trapped with Balor. Not that he was one of the originals. He hadn't been kidding earlier when he said he'd lived a long time. I was almost two thousand years old, which meant he was over twice my age.

I swallowed over the lump in my throat. Well, shit.

"You're surprised." His brows furrowed together as he tilted his head. "Why?"

My eyes snapped from the flames to meet his stare.

I wasn't an easy person to read, and yet he had known what I was feeling so easily. Unease rippled through me, and I adjusted the threat level Niall represented.

"I still have another question," I said instead of answering him. He frowned but didn't argue. "Do you still serve Balor?"

I kept my eyes on him, searching for any signs that he was

lying. I may not be able to read minds, but I was good at picking up the cues that people made with their expression and body language.

Although, Niall was already demonstrating that he could read me well, which meant he probably also knew how to lie to me. The smart thing to do would be to get information out of him and then dump his body somewhere no one would find it. Nemain may have spared his life before, but it's not like she offered him safehaven, so clearly she didn't care about him that much.

"I'm not with them anymore," he said quietly. "I no longer serve Balor, and I never gave a shit about that asshole Lir."

I couldn't help but notice the way his eyes darkened at the mention of Lir, hinting at some type of history between them.

"You have no reason to believe or trust me, I understand. Just like I understand that you're planning on killing me once you get the answers you want because of the threat I am to not only you but those you care about. I don't blame you; I'd likely do the same in your situation. Just thought you should know where I stand with Balor."

Every part of me wanted to reach for the dagger at my belt and thrust it into his heart. Not because he was a fae devourer. Not because he had attacked and tried to kill my friend.

But because he saw me so clearly when so few did. There was no greater threat than that.

His eyes flicked down to where my hand had fallen to my side, but he didn't seem concerned. If anything, he seemed eager.

Slowly I pulled my hand away and let it rest on my knee. I'd seen the same expression on his face earlier when we'd been fighting. It wasn't the exhilarated look that Nemain got when we sparred. There was something about Niall's expression that set my nerves on end.

Whatever the look was, it slid off his face and was replaced by his charming smile.

I didn't call him on it because I didn't understand what it meant. And I didn't want him to read too much into how much attention I was giving his handsome face.

Instead, I said nothing as Niall cautiously reached out and set the bone, still wrapped with some meat, in front of Gunnar. The wolf eyed it suspiciously before sniffing it. He pondered it for a few more seconds before using one large paw to push it over to Viggo.

The skogkatt snatched it up and leapt into the air, bounding upward as if he was jumping from one invisible lily pad to the other before disappearing into the trees.

I'd seen Nemain's grimalkin, Jinx, do the same thing multiple times. Viggo and Jinx might hate each other, but they were both cats and preferred to eat their meals in high places given the chance.

"I believe it's my turn to ask a question?" Niall said carefully.

I nodded and took another big bite so I had time to stall in case he asked me something I needed to skirt around the truth on. Unlike the fae, I didn't have to worry about my magic punishing me for lying, but I still didn't like to do it. Still, I was more than willing to offer partial truths.

His blue eyes fell on me, brimming with curiosity. "Why were you surprised earlier when I told you I'd been with Balor from the beginning?"

I blinked at the unexpected question. I assumed he'd ask something more relevant, maybe about my hammer or about Nemain.

"It's been a while since I met someone older than me," I said slowly. "Aside from some other valkyries and a few Asgardians. There are some daemons around that are my age or older, but I don't know them very well."

And Guillveg. But I didn't feel like getting into her now, and it was none of his business anyway.

"What are you?" The question slipped out before I could pull it back. Damn it. There were more important questions I should be asking right now, but my curiosity got the better of me.

"Sciathán." He said with a smile that failed to reach his eyes. "We were once a powerful warrior race in the fae realms. Not as magically gifted as the sidhe or merfolk, but we were very close with nature, and she would whisper her secrets to us. Tell us where the best prey was located. If a storm was coming in. Where a river flowed through the forest."

"Do you still hear these whispers even with your devourer nature?"

The false smile slipped from his face. "I believe it's my turn to ask a question."

I waved a hand at him to continue while I finished the remaining meat on my stick before tossing it into the fire.

Sciathán. I filed away that word for later. Maybe Nemain's friend Kaysea would know who or what the sciathán were. If not, Nemain was on a first-name basis with the Unseelie Queen now. Surely, she would know.

"Why are you in this realm?" he asked.

"My friends had business in this realm," I said vaguely. "A seraph general had something they needed, and I helped provide a distraction."

"Ah, yes. That rather epic throwdown outside one of the cities," Niall mused. "Based on the grumblings I've heard, the seraphim are still really pissed off about that. I don't think Lir was impressed by how well they got their asses handed to them either."

The corner of his lips quirked up, and I fought to keep the satisfied grin off my face. It had been one hell of a fight, and I'd enjoyed every second of it.

"That doesn't explain why you're still here."

I debated how much to tell him and then just decided to come out with it. I'd bested him in a fight already, and I was confident I'd be able to do so again if needed.

He was more likely to offer me good information if he felt I was doing the same in return. Fair's fair.

I'd already decided that he wouldn't be walking away from me while I was in this realm. The only thing I had left to determine was whether he'd still be breathing in the morning or if I'd force him to travel with me until I could deliver him to Nemain and let her decide his fate.

"We had reason to believe that Balor was recruiting the seraphim to work for him," I said evenly, making sure my tone remained neutral. "He's already recruited a few other species, so logically it makes sense for him to use the seraphim as well. They're powerful and have a bone to pick with both the fae and daemons."

"What about the children?"

"What do you mean?" I frowned at him.

Niall stared at me for a few beats. "Did you know the seraphim were stealing children from other realms?"

"Other realms?" I pursed my lips as I thought of the humans in the pens.

Most of them had been children or in their late teens, which I thought was a little unusual at the time but assumed they were keeping the adults somewhere else.

"I've seen the holding pens in some of their cities," I said slowly. "Do you know something about them?"

Niall stared at me, and I knew he was once again seeing far more in my expression than I wanted him to. "Not enough," he grunted. "I saw them bring in a large group a couple months ago, but I'm not sure from where. They were all young, though. Humans aren't all that familiar to me, but I don't think any of them were past their first decade."

"I've seen adults here."

I racked my brain, trying to remember the age distribution of the last group of humans I'd spotted. The oldest among them had probably been in their mid-thirties?

I added, "But humans have quick and short lives. It's possible they came to this realm as children and have managed to survive this long."

"Not all of them," he said darkly. "They've been conducting hunts."

A muscle along my jaw ticked. I knew what he meant. They'd done the same in the human realm before they were exiled from it.

The seraphim were predators, and while they enjoyed going after more dangerous prey, the humans provided a fun source of entertainment for them. They especially liked hunting children. I wasn't particularly compassionate towards humans as a whole, but slaughtering children of any species was pretty fucked up.

Magic sparked from the hammer at my side, sensing my rage. Niall's eyes slid to the weapon and back to me, but he didn't ask about it.

I stared at it while I worked on calming the tempest of wrath swirling inside me. Part of me itched to pick it up and fly straight to the seraphim camp where I could unleash its magic on them all. There were over a thousand seraphs there, and I could end their lives in less than a minute.

It would only cost me a piece of my soul.

Faint lines glowed along the sides of the hammer, lighting up glyphs as the magic called to me. The void I carried deep within my soul beckoned me to answer it.

Bryn's solemn grey eyes flashed in my mind.

She needed me. I couldn't do this.

I had barely managed to claw my way back last time I had truly wielded the hammer.

With agonizing slowness, I turned away from the hammer and focused back on the fae who had remained quiet while I had my inner battle.

"Why are you here, Niall?" I asked, my voice harsh and raspy.

"Technically, I think it's my turn to ask a question."

"Game's over."

"Fair enough." He leaned back, gazing up at the trees. "I needed somewhere to nap. And it was a very nice tree."

I frowned, confused by his answer, and then I remembered where he had been at the start of our encounter. "Not why you were in the tree," I growled. "Why are you in this fucking realm?"

"That's not what you asked." He shrugged. "I answered your question."

Now he chose to act like a typical fae. My annoyance boiled over into anger. The hammer leapt into my hand, and I surged to my feet. Even if I didn't use it to its true potential, it was still a good weapon. "Don't get cute with me, fae. Answer the godsdamned question."

In one smooth motion, Niall rolled onto his feet, but he didn't draw a weapon.

Strands of his dark hair slipped free, framing his face before he brushed them back behind his ears. Once again, his eyes fell on my hammer, and I wondered how much of its magic he could see or feel.

I really needed to replenish the concealment spell on it to hide its true nature, but there was nothing I could do about that now. Originally, I'd disguised it as a battle ax, which truth be told was usually my preferred weapon, but it had been less than pleased by that and rapidly burned away the illusion.

"When Nemain spared my life, I had the pleasure of meeting her mother. She shoved me through a gateway with a warning to stay the fuck away from her daughter." His dark eyebrows crept up. "Not a lot of people scare me, but The Morrigan is definitely on that list now."

Having met Nemain's mother, I could understand that. She wasn't as powerful as her mate, The Erlking, but she was every bit as ruthless. Maybe even more so.

The two of them together were formidable; even I wasn't sure if I'd be able to walk away from that fight.

"She sent me to a fae realm, but not one of the main ones. It was remote and isolated enough that no one bothered me." He paused for a moment before continuing, "I've spent the last few thousand years locked away in that realm the fae queens trapped us in. It was only a year ago that I came here with my unit. Nothing is the same, and I don't really know my way around."

Niall's hands clenched and unclenched at his sides, displaying a rare moment of frustration instead of the easy grins and blasé attitude he typically wore.

"I didn't know what to do, but I knew I couldn't stay in the fae realm, even though it wasn't very populated. Sooner or later, another fae would realize my magic wasn't right. It took a while, but I eventually found one of the gateways they had set up in that realm. It was barely guarded, which was rather care-less of them. It was easy enough to slip back to the human world."

"Why?" I kept my expression neutral even as a tinge of empathy flickered in me. It'd been hard for me to adjust to being an exile, but at least I had known my way around the various realms.

Niall had disappeared from this world long ago, only to return and find everything different with not a familiar face in sight. Nobody would ever accuse me of being particularly social. But even I couldn't imagine moving through a world that had once been familiar but was now full of strangers.

He hesitated, as if trying to choose his words carefully. "I came back to find Nemain."

"The Morrigan doesn't make idle threats." I shook my head and lowered my assessment of Niall's intelligence. "If she found out you were going after her daughter, she would have ripped you apart. Slowly."

"I wasn't 'going after' Nemain." He glared at me stubbornly. "I just wanted to speak with her. But when I made it to the town she lived in, I saw some of Lir's men and I wanted to know what they were up to.

"When they opened a gateway, I dove through it before it snapped shut. Despite what you think, I took the threat from The Morrigan quite seriously. I thought that maybe if I could offer information about what Lir was up to, she'd overlook the whole me trying to kill her daughter thing."

I gave him a doubtful look. He was definitely dumber than I had thought.

"Yeah," he chuckled. "It sounds pretty stupid when I say it out loud, doesn't it? She would have thanked me for the information and then sliced my head off."

I snorted. "She wouldn't have thanked you."

"Alright, I concede my plan was flawed, but I wasn't really sure what to do. Most of my people followed Balor, and I suspect the queens killed off whoever was left in punishment." His throat bobbed as he swallowed. "I don't have anyone left. The fae who follow the queens will kill me if they discover me here. I've deserted Balor's army. My options are pretty limited these days."

More sympathy crept into me, but I was careful to keep my face blank. I was all too familiar with what it felt like to be an outsider who was no longer wanted by your own people.

But I hadn't had a choice, Niall's words implied that he had willingly followed Balor, at least in the beginning.

"So you followed Lir and his men here," I said. "Then what?"

"Oh, they caught me." He shrugged one shoulder.

"What?" I took a step away from him and hefted my hammer a little higher. Had he led them to me? Was that why he was so keen on having a conversation with me? Just to get me to lower my guard?

"It's not what you think!" he said quickly and then paused as he thought about it. "Actually, it's exactly what you think… sort of."

"Explain," I commanded, narrowing my eyes.

"Some of Lir's men recognized me. All of my unit died in that fae realm where I encountered Nemain, and everyone had assumed I'd died with them. I was locked up until they figured out what was going on. Then you lot attacked the seraphim city, and a few rumors spread about there still being a valkyrie in this realm—one who wielded a hammer of great power. I've always been an excellent tracker, and Lir decided he had a use for me after all."

"So you are still working for Balor." My fingers tightened around the hammer's handle. I knew I should have bashed his head in earlier instead of letting his handsome face and charming words cloud my judgement.

"No." Niall shook his head firmly and raised his hands. "Lir's arrogance is quite possibly his greatest weakness. He always thinks he's the smartest person in the room, and definitely smarter than some sciatháin tracker."

Once again, I noted the way he practically spat Lir's name. Definitely some bad blood there.

"Go on."

"I swore on my life that I would find you and bring you back to the fae devourers."

"Nemain and Kalen are both fae devourers." Technically,

Nemain was also a feline shifter, but fae and devourer blood ran through her veins.

"Indeed, they are." Niall grinned.

Both my eyebrows raised. "And Lir didn't call you on that bullshit?"

"Like I said, his arrogance is his greatest weakness." He shrugged. "So… do we have a deal? I'll help you with whatever it is you're up to here, and you'll speak on my behalf to Nemain?"

I thought about it. Assuming this wasn't all a trap, Niall could provide us with some valuable information. There was so much we didn't know about the magic wielded by the fae who followed Balor. They'd all been twisted by devourer magic, but we'd only fought against a few of them.

Other information like how the army was structured and how many types of devourers they had under their control would be good to know as well. Even if Niall wasn't privy to the plans Balor and Lir had in place, the general knowledge he'd picked up as a former soldier in their army would be immensely helpful.

Assuming we could trust him. My instincts were telling me he was on the level, but I'd been wrong before.

"I'll think about it and let you know in the morning," I finally settled on saying. "I'd suggest you get some rest."

"Not gonna stab me in the back while I'm sleeping, are you?" he asked teasingly.

"I'm a valkyrie." I slid him a sidelong glance and allowed myself a small smile. "I'd stab you in the front."

Chapter Four

A WET TONGUE sliding across my cheek woke me up shortly before sunrise.

"Ack! Enough, Gunnar!" I sputtered.

The wolf wagged his tail before leaping away and doing the same thing to Viggo, who took it even worse than I had.

The two of them tumbled across the clearing, with Viggo letting out pissed-off snarls and Gunnar mock growling in return. Most of the time, Gunnar played the role of stoic wolf companion, but sometimes he would embrace his inner pup and have some fun. Typically at Viggo's expense.

I glanced up at the tree I'd originally noticed Niall in and wasn't surprised to see him stretched out across one of the thicker branches, leaning his back against the trunk.

"Did you seriously sleep up there?" The branch he was on was wide, but still… if he rolled over, his ass would have fallen a good twenty feet.

"I like trees." He yawned and stretched before flipping off the branch and landing gracefully on his feet. "Besides, the wolf was determined to watch me all night, and it was a bit unnerving to sleep with him glaring at me from a few feet away."

"Fair enough," I replied, not at all apologizing for Gunnar's behavior.

Niall and I might have come to an understanding last night, but that didn't mean I trusted him enough to sleep near him unguarded. Viggo, Gunnar, and I would be trading watch duty for however long Niall traveled with us.

"So, what have you decided?" Niall asked as he dug through his traveling pack and pulled out a sack of berries.

He took a handful and then passed it over to me. I peered into the bag and looked at the bright blue berries. Taking a handful for myself, I tossed the bag back to him. I had some dried meat packed away, but I wasn't going to turn down fresh fruit.

I popped one of the berries into my mouth and enjoyed the tart flavor exploding across my tongue. He must have found these in this realm; maybe we could gather some more today while we were flying around.

Niall let me savor the berries instead of pushing me for an answer. His blue eyes lit up at my clear enjoyment at the food he'd offered.

"You'll accompany me as I continue to glean information on the seraphim," I said. "We'll follow this group for a little bit longer before returning to the human realm."

"So you'll speak to Nemain on my behalf?" Niall asked, his eyes lighting up with hope.

"I'll encourage her to not kill you on sight and listen to what you have to say," I clarified. "The rest of it is her decision." I was fairly certain that Nemain wouldn't kill him since she had spared his life before. Badb, however, was another matter.

"How much longer do you plan on staying here?"

I pursed my lips as I stared in the direction where the seraphim were camped.

"I'd like to know where this group is heading and if possible maybe spy on Lir if he's still around. Either way, the seraphim have clearly gone unchecked for too long, and it's time for the fae queens to do something about it."

Niall stiffened slightly before attempting to cover it up with a nonchalant shrug. "Very well."

I eyed him, debating whether I should share this information or not. Finally, I decided that even if Niall *did* prove to be an enemy, which I didn't think was the case, this wasn't a secret.

He'd find out on his own soon enough.

"You should know that things have changed for Nemain since you last saw her. Between her and the fae queens. Specifically, between her and the Unseelie Queen."

"Oh?" He set the bag full of delicious berries down and pulled his leather vest off the branch it was draped over, tugging it on. His fingers nimbly laced up the sides until it was snuggly fitted against his upper body.

Like me, he'd slept with his boots and the rest of his clothes on. The vest was the only thing he'd tossed during the night.

"She not only belongs to the Unseelie Court now, but she's also their Knight." It still sounded insane to hear it out loud.

Nemain had always hated the fae and their bullshit politics. Now, she was at the center of it all.

I felt bad for my friend. She'd done it because it was the only way to protect Finn, and I would have done the same in her situation. But willingly or not, Nemain's life was radically changed now.

"Shit," he swore, lifting his head towards the sky and squeezing his eyes shut. "I was really hoping to stay as far away from those bitches as possible."

"The queens?" I studied the profile of his face, seeing the

faint lines of anger at the corner of his mouth and eyes. "Is it because you're a traitor?"

His head snapped towards me, those brilliant sky-blue eyes now alight with fury.

My fingers itched to grab my hammer, but I held still. This was the most emotion I'd seen from Niall since we'd met. The laid-back fae male was gone, and only the warrior stood before me now.

"I followed *my king*," he snarled with barely contained rage. "Because for all his faults, he never looked down on the sciatháin. The rest of the sidhe, *including* his sisters, treated us like we were less simply because we didn't have the right type of magic. It's why the sciatháin joined king's army in droves. It was the only place in the fae realms where we were respected or valued. You never heard of the sciatháin until you met me. Any guesses as to why?"

Tension coiled its way through my body as I took in the pain and wrath etched into Niall's features.

I didn't have to guess what had happened to his people.

While I preferred to stay out of the fae realms, I had spent plenty of time there over my lifetime. If there was a skilled and powerful group of warriors, I would have known about them.

The fae queens were ruthless. They had to be to pull off the coup against their brother and hold onto power all this time. The sciatháin who remained in the fae realms after they trapped Balor and his army would have been a threat to them.

Threats were annihilated.

"I see you've come to the same conclusion I have," Niall said darkly. "I heard no whispers of the sciatháin while I was in the fae realms, and unless you're an incredibly talented liar, you've never heard of them before you met me. The queens killed my people, and Balor has twisted what remains of us."

"I'm sorry." The two words came out as a hoarse whisper.

My people might still exist, but they were lost to me. I knew what it was like to be alone in the world.

"It is what it is." The underlying anger was gone from his voice, but his face still held touches of it.

"Such is life." I gave him a humorless smile, and Niall cocked his head. "It's a phrase Nemain always says. Well, she says it in French, c'est la vie."

Niall grimaced and touched the space behind his right ear. "These translation marks are strange," he muttered. "I never needed one before because I spoke all the fae languages, but we received them right away when we got to the human realm. Still not used to feeling the magic spark occasionally."

I smiled. "It'll become second nature eventually to understand the nature of the magic. Assuming you stick around, you'll probably want to learn the daemon language and a few others. As good as the magic is behind the marks, some things still get lost in translation."

"Daemon…" That playful smile spread across his lips, and the tension I'd been feeling slid away at seeing it again. "Yet another species I have yet to encounter. It's been a long time since I've had so many new things to see… It's an odd feeling."

He held out the bag of berries, and I eagerly took a handful from it.

"Well, Nemain spends quite a bit of time with the daemons, so you'll get your chance to meet one soon enough." I paused to shove some berries into my mouth and closed my eyes in enjoyment.

They were like a mix of blueberries and raspberries but a little more sour. The climate here was similar enough to the realm I was currently living in, so maybe I could grab a cutting of whatever plant they grew on and try planting it in my garden.

Juice ran down the corner of my mouth and down my chin. I raised my hand to wipe it off, but Niall beat me to it.

My eyes flew open as he swiped a finger across my face and handed over the bag with the rest of the berries. I snatched it from him and opened my mouth to berate him about touching me when he licked the juices off his finger.

My eyes tracked the movement, and I was acutely aware of certain parts of my body coming to full attention.

"So we're going to follow the war party or whatever it is?" he asked after he was done cleaning off his fingers. If he noticed my rapt attention on his movements, he didn't let it show.

"Yes," I said, careful to keep my tone even.

I was attracted to Niall.

It wasn't a big deal, nor was it all that surprising. He was good-looking with a strong build and was skilled in a fight.

So, *exactly* my type.

But I wasn't one to just give into my sexual desires. There was a time and place for that, and this was neither.

So I locked down that part of myself and promised it I'd give it some attention when we were out of here. Maybe find a daemon or something to have a tumble with. Someone who I could enjoy for a night and then move on.

My life was already complex; I didn't need to add a complicated love life too.

"Alright." Niall picked up his travel pack. "I'm ready whenever you are."

I cocked my head at him. "How exactly have you been following me?"

That thought should have occurred to me sooner, but with everything going on, I hadn't pondered how exactly Niall had been keeping up with me and the seraphim considering we spent all day flying. I hadn't seen any horses or transportation creatures in this realm, either.

Nemain mentioned that Lir had several large, winged creatures with him. Maybe Niall had procured one of those? That would explain the dark creature I thought I saw flying away that one night.

Niall grabbed the now empty bag from me and dropped it into the leather pack before slipping the straps over his shoulders so that the pack rested against his chest instead of his back.

He grinned at me as large black wings burst out of his back. "I think I'll be able to keep up just fine."

I took a step forward before I caught myself and stopped. If my wings were the golden rays of the sun, Niall's were the inky darkness of night.

They looked soft, and I wanted to run my fingers across them, but it was rude to touch another valkyrie's wings without permission. I didn't know how the sciatháin felt about it, but even then, it seemed like a line I shouldn't cross with Niall considering I was already attracted to him.

"Glamour?" I asked curiously.

He hadn't shifted; the wings had simply not been there one moment, and then there the next.

I could make my wings invisible, but they were still physically there. If Niall could do something similar, I would have felt them while we were fighting.

"Yes," he said, stretching his wings out wide. They were bigger than mine, I noted begrudgingly. "The sciatháin don't have much in the way of magic, as I said before. But we received a little bit of a boost when Balor mixed devourer magic with ours. We're still not particularly good at glamouring, but most of us have at least figured out how to hide our wings."

I walked around him to get a better look. They were actually pretty similar to seraphim wings with their fluffy feathers, but Niall's were black and a bit smoother.

"Weak spot in a fight?" I guessed.

"Yes," he admitted. "Not all of us have spears we can shoot out of our wings."

"Don't be jealous," I said with a grin before going to pack up my own supplies.

It would be at least a few weeks before I could pull that move again; the feathers needed to grow back, but I wasn't going to tell him that.

Instead, I asked, "What else can you do?"

A cryptic smile spread across his lips. "Tell me about the hammer, and I'll tell you."

Not a chance. I didn't say those words out loud, but the look I gave him clearly conveyed them because he let out a low laugh in response.

"Try to keep up." I shot into the sky, Viggo and Gunnar right behind me. Within seconds, Niall flew above me and hung back a little like a dark shadow.

Chapter Five

THE NEXT THREE days were the same. Fly. Stop. Eat. Sleep. Repeat. Niall and I sparred, while Gunnar and Viggo hunted.

Having such a worthy opponent was exhilarating, and I understood why Nemain had been so impressed by his swordsmanship. Our matches always ended in a draw with both of us sweating as the ground soaked up our blood.

We were careful not to deal any serious wounds, but both of us seemed to crave carving up a little skin in the game.

Part of me knew I should be wary of how easily Niall was slipping past my defenses. I was just a means to an end for him, a way for him to meet with Nemain and not be cut down within seconds. And he was the same for me, someone who had insider information that could be useful.

And yet I found myself enjoying his company more and more each day.

It unsettled me, but every time I tried to put up walls between us again, Niall would do something to tear them down leaving me feeling bewildered.

It was all very confusing. But our time together was limited, so I told myself that it didn't really matter. Once we got what we needed from the other, we'd be parting ways. Nemain might decide to help him out, but it's not like she'd add him to her merry band of misfits. Right?

I frowned. Shit. Nemain *was* starting to make a habit of collecting strays…

"Don't know why you're upset." Niall rotated his shoulder and winced. "You were clearly the winner of that match."

The seraphim had cut their flight short today and we'd sparred while they were setting up camp. After he'd slashed my ribs pretty good, I'd dropped my hammer and grabbed his arm. He'd been so shocked by the move that he didn't respond in time to keep me from spinning us around to pick up speed before flinging him into a tree.

His shoulder had taken the brunt of the hit, and I was pretty sure I heard something snap. Point for me.

My frown flipped into a smirk. "You good?"

He did his best to glower at me but finally gave up, and a bright smile lit up his face. "I'm doing great. Who doesn't love getting slammed into a tree?"

I rolled my eyes even as I let out a low laugh. "There's something wrong with you."

"That's very likely," he agreed. "I'm going to go rinse off before sunset and the heat of the day leaves us."

"Good idea." I pulled my shirt away from my skin with a grimace. There hadn't been anywhere to bathe these past couple days, so I had several layers of dirt, sweat, and dried blood on me.

Thank the gods. Viggo wrinkled his nose from where he was lying stretched out in the sun a dozen feet away. *I can smell you from here.*

Gunnar let out a small woof in agreement.

"Rude," I muttered, crossing my arms.

Niall glanced back and forth between the two curiously but didn't say anything.

He knew that Viggo could speak telepathically because the skogkatt had threatened to slice his balls off and feed them to the wolf if he so much as looked at me the wrong way. That was the one and only time Viggo had deigned to speak with him.

New people made Viggo wary, and it usually took him a while to warm up to them, if he ever did. He still only spoke to Nemain if he absolutely had to, but that was mostly because of her bond with Jinx.

Apparently, skogkatts and grimalkins didn't mix well.

"I take it the two of you are going to stay here then?" I grabbed my canteen and took a long swig of water, flinching slightly when the movement tugged on my ribs.

"Do you need to wrap that?" Niall gestured to where blood was seeping through my shirt on my side.

"No." I tossed the canteen down next to my bag. "I'll chant a healing spell once I'm cleaned off. It'll heal up in an hour."

Niall nodded, his features still creased in concern, but followed me towards the river we'd spotted while looking for a place to camp. We spent the short walk in companionable silence. While I wouldn't call my time in this realm enjoyable exactly, I did like the forests. Most of the trees were some type of pine, and they gave off a rich, sappy scent.

Small birds with bright green and yellow feathers let out quick chirps followed by long whistles as they flitted about from branch to branch. Most of the mammals here were shy, but I'd spotted a few tree dwellers that looked like a cross between a raccoon from the human realm and the coastal bears from Vanaheim.

Every time I'd seen them, their masked faces had been covered in berry juice, and they'd scurried away without a hint of aggression.

Even I had to admit they were kind of adorable.

The sound of rushing water soon reached my ears, and I

was suddenly really eager to reach it. The cool water would feel wonderful against my sore muscles, and I desperately wanted to clean my clothes. I smelled *rank*.

"Let's find a spot that still has a decent amount of coverage." I glanced up at the forest canopy that was thin enough for me to see large chunks of sky. "The seraphim camp is at least a mile away, but there's always a chance a scout could fly over us."

"When we reach the river, let's head west," Niall said. "If I remember correctly, the trees will thicken up that way."

Niall's memory proved to be spot-on, and less than ten minutes later we found the perfect spot. The crystal-clear water flowed around several bends, slowing down the current, and large trees stretched over the river, granting us privacy from anyone flying overhead.

"Finally." I strode over to a large flat rock near the water's edge and began shrugging off my weapons. The daggers and their sheaths were first, followed by the hammer. I unwrapped the band holding my braids back and redid it so that they sat in a bun on the top of my head. "I suggest not being between me and the hammer in case I have to call it to me. Unless you don't value your head." I gave Niall a pointed look.

"You know it kills me that you won't tell me anything about it, right?" he complained. "What type of hammer comes when you call it? That's super weir—"

I looked over my shoulder from where I stood in the river, the water up to my waist and my clothes piled up on some of the large boulders that rose up above the surface. Niall was staring at me wide-eyed with his mouth slightly ajar.

"What?" I quirked an eyebrow at him. "Never seen a naked valkyrie before?"

His mouth clamped shut.

"Can't say that I have… Thank you for continuing to grant me new experiences."

He remained rooted in place, eyes flicking back and forth between the ground in front of him and me. My lips curled up. Apparently, the charming and calming sciathán was embarrassed by a bit of nudity. How quaint.

"So, you just going to stand there or…?"

"I… uhh…" he stammered. "I assumed we'd be bathing in different parts of the river."

I shrugged and turned away from him, taking a few more steps until the water covered my chest and then spun back around to face him.

"You're welcome to go further upstream. Just make sure to stay somewhere covered."

"You really don't care if I strip right here and get in there with you?" He chewed on his bottom lip. Even from here, I caught his throat bob as he swallowed.

I chuckled. "While I haven't seen a naked sciathán before, the rest of you seems pretty ordinary, so I don't think you're going to have anything I haven't seen before."

"Not sure how I feel about being called *ordinary*," he muttered but moved to the rock where all my weapons were laid out to start shedding his clothes.

"The valkyries have never been shy about nudity, nor have the Asgardians or Vanir." I stretched my wings out in the water, enjoying the feel of the current rushing through the feathers. "Plus, I've spent a lot of time around Nemain and as a shifter, she *really* doesn't give a single fuck about nudity."

"I don't have a problem with nudity," he insisted as he tugged off his boots. "I have a problem with you."

Excuse me? The amused grin slid off my face.

"Well, sorry, but I'm not going anywhere. You can find your own damn spot in the river." I leaned back and let myself float on my back, my wings beating slowly beneath the water to keep me afloat.

"Fuck." He slapped a hand over his face. "That came out

wrong. I just meant that I wasn't prepared to see you naked. You're the most glorious thing I've ever seen, Sigrun."

Oh. I swallowed and let my arms drift out to the side as I continued to tread water. Now it was my turn to be speechless.

"You're forgiven for the rude comment," I finally said. "You're welcome to bathe here with me or somewhere else. But we both need to clean ourselves and our clothes, otherwise Viggo will complain all night."

"Fair enough." He grinned, and the easy camaraderie we had instantly fell back in place.

Until he pulled off his shirt and began to pull down his pants. At that point, my heart started hammering in my chest, and I immediately spun around to face the other side of the river.

When I slowly drifted back around to face him, Niall was already in the river, the water up to his waist.

A few thick, ropey scars cut across his chest. I not only wanted to know what had caused them, but I was also dying to trail my fingers across the scars and down the hard planes of his stomach.

My gaze snagged at the water line, and suddenly I couldn't decide if I was glad I hadn't watched him get into the water or if that had been the worst mistake of my life.

"You good, valkyrie?" A lopsided grin was stamped on Niall's face, as if he could read my thoughts.

"Of course," I replied in a voice that was slightly deeper than normal. "We should wash our clothes and set them out to dry while the sun is still out."

"Sure." A heated glint entered his eyes. "You first."

My still damp shirt clung to my back, but I'd waited as long as I could for it to dry. If we'd stayed in that river much longer,

I was fairly certain I would have done something foolish. Niall was a devourer fae who had defected from Balor's army, but I only had his word on that.

Getting involved with him, even just for a physical release, was a bad idea. Particularly while I was in enemy territory.

After we'd finished up at the river, I'd checked in with Viggo and Gunnar. Much to my annoyance, Viggo had gone off on his own to scope out the seraphim camp, which had apparently grown in number. The four of us had immediately gone to investigate.

"That has to be at least the fifth new group to join them in the last day," Niall noted quietly from where he crouched beside me.

The two of us and Gunnar were hidden behind a large fallen tree. Viggo was perched on top. He hadn't activated his invisibility magic, but his brown coat blended in well with the bark.

"There must be close to five thousand of them now." My eyes skimmed over the camp, roughly adding up the numbers.

Like us, they didn't bother with tents. The seraphs simply laid out bedrolls and dropped their traveling packs on them and sometimes their weapons before wandering over to one of the many bonfires.

I murmured, "They must have stopped early because this was the only clearing large enough to fit them all." My brows bunched together.

This wasn't just a war party; this was an *army*. Where were they going?

I'm going to wander around the camp and see if I can pick up anything useful, Viggo said. *Make sure the dog saves me some food.*

The skogkatt leapt down from the tree and trotted off towards where the seraphim were gathered, his coat shimmering as he turned invisible.

I wanted to call him back, but I bit my tongue. Skoggkat

magic was more limited than mine, but their ability to turn invisible was stronger. There was no chance of the seraphim spotting him. It was harder for me to lurk in the camp because even though I couldn't be seen, I could be felt. Wings, even tucked tightly, could be a nuisance at times.

He'll be fine, I told Gunnar as he stared off after Viggo, concern in his eyes. *Why don't you go get something to eat while I find us a place to rest?*

The wolf took off on silent paws as he dashed through the forest. I headed in the same direction, and Niall followed close behind.

Eventually, we emerged in a small clearing that would do for us to camp in for the night. There wasn't enough space to create a fire, and even with my magic making it smokeless, I didn't want to risk a seraph scout flying above us and spotting the flames.

Speaking of being seen, I cast the invisibility spell over my wings to hide their golden feathers.

Niall frowned at my back and the wings he could no longer see.

"They're still there," I said dryly.

"I know." He gave me a lopsided grin. "I'd just prefer that you didn't have to hide such a glorious part of you."

Once again, I was thankful that I didn't have Bryn's tendency to blush wildly. I felt my cheeks warm a little bit, but with my dark complexion, it wasn't nearly as noticeable on me as it was on my young apprentice with her lightly tanned skin. When Bryn blushed, she practically turned bright red from head to toe, much to Elisa's delight.

Niall's grin blossomed into a full-blown smile. Damn it. His ability to read me had only gotten better since we'd been traveling together.

"You've been in this realm longer than me," I said, redirecting the focus away from me acting like a lovestruck teenager. "Any ideas on where they might be heading?"

"I was actually going to talk to you about that." He pulled his leather bag off and dropped it on the ground. "We're pretty close to where I originally followed Lir and his unit through the gateway. There's a large city nearby, and I suspect that's where they're going. From what I saw when flying around this region, it's the only city large enough that makes sense for an army this size to use as a base."

I mulled this over for a moment before nodding. "How big is the city, and what do you know of it?"

"Not much." He shrugged. "I was immediately hauled away and locked in a room until Lir gave me the task of finding you, but I saw some of it when I flew away. It's rather massive. I'd guess there are over a hundred thousand seraphim living there, and it's extremely well-defended. But I couldn't tell you the layout or where Lir is within it."

"It's been challenging enough sneaking through the smaller cities. If the city is as populated as you think, we'll have to be extremely careful about navigating through it." I mulled over the information before lifting my gaze to Niall. "Do you know how to get to the city from here?"

Niall nodded. "We could probably get there in a day and a half if we took minimal breaks."

I chewed on the inside of my cheek. Niall had already admitted that Lir had caught him and only released him to capture me.

Given that the sciatháin had in all likelihood been annihilated by the fae queens, Niall would have no loyalty to them. Logically, it made sense that he was still working for Balor and that this was a trap.

He didn't have to worry about defeating me in a fight if he just got me to go to the city where Lir was and betrayed me there.

But I felt like I could trust him, and in my nearly two thousand years of existence, my instincts had rarely been wrong. I'd ignored them during Ragnarok because I didn't like what they were telling me. And there were times, like when Nemain would pester me about something, that I wouldn't always listen to them right away… and I always regretted it.

Niall had done nothing to make me doubt his word over the last few days.

And I found myself enjoying his company more and more, which was a problem in itself that I'd have to deal with.

Later. That was a problem for later.

"Then we'll rest tonight and leave a few hours before sunrise," I said, having come to a decision. "The seraphim are probably heading there now, in which case I'd rather get there before them. It'll be hard enough to navigate around the city as it is."

"It's possible they're going somewhere else," Niall warned. "I'm only guessing about them going to the city based on their direction. But I haven't traveled anywhere south of it, so I don't know what else is there."

"It's worth a shot. Especially if Lir or any of his followers are there. We might be able to get specific information on what he's offering the seraphim and what his plans for them are."

He nodded. "Very well. I'll take first watch tonight if you want to rest after eating."

Niall set about pulling out water and food from his bag, including to my delight some berries that we'd collected earlier. I did the same as I watched him through veiled lashes. His tone had been light and even, but I was getting better at reading him too.

The muscles along his jaw had tightened at the mention of Lir's name, and he was being very careful with his movements, as if he was working hard to keep them casual.

"What's the deal with you and Li—" My words were cut off as something slammed into me.

Agony laced up my side. My back crunched as it collided with a tree, but I pushed through the pain and leapt to my feet to take on my would-be attacker.

"Sigrun!" Niall roared.

A large beast rose in front of me on two stout legs, its body covered in pitch-black scales. Putrid breath slammed into me as it opened its maw, revealing rows of sharp yellow teeth before it dove straight for my face.

Chapter Six

INSTEAD OF DIVING to either side, I crouched as low as I could, tucking my wings in tight. The tree cracked as the beast's front legs slammed into its sides, sharp claws digging into the bark. Jaws snapped shut in the space where my head had been mere seconds ago.

In one smooth motion, I rotated my hammer so that the handle was pointed straight up. The magic within it was bound to my will, and it knew what I wanted.

The silver cap on the handle's end molded into a sharp point, and I thrust it upward. The creature shrieked as the handle went straight through its lower jaw and into its brain. Magic sparked, and a bolt of lightning ripped through its head.

The ear-piercing cry abruptly cut off, and I barely managed to pull the hammer free and duck to the side before the beast collapsed in a heap.

The smell of ozone and another foul stench filled the air. Within seconds, the monster decomposed until it was nothing but bones and dust. I scattered the bones until I found what I'd been looking for. My fingers plucked the shiny black scale that was as wide as my palm and almost as long as my hand from the remains.

"What the fuck is that?" Niall ran over to me, his panicked eyes searching my body for injuries.

"It's a nidling," I spat as I held up the black scale. "Long ago, there was a beast called Nidhogg. She wreaked all sorts of havoc across the realms before she was finally slain. But pieces of her went missing after her death, including a good amount of her scales. The nidlings are warped copies of her that are created with dark magic."

Finally coming to the conclusion that I hadn't been injured, Niall's stance eased a little, and he turned an examining stare to what was left of the nidling.

His brow furrowed. "Why was it here?"

"It's a long story." I straightened and moved away from the tree to give myself more space. "But they always hunt in a pack of three."

His gaze slid back to me. "I'd like to hear this story someday, valkyrie."

"I'll think about it," I said tightly.

Gunnar's deep growl echoed through the clearing.

The other two nidlings are coming in fast! Viggo warned.

The hammer instantly leapt into my palm. Niall pulled out his sword and dagger and took up a fighting stance a few feet to my side.

"Is your hammer the only thing capable of killing them?"

"Your devourer magic might work," I said instead of answering him.

The muscles of his jaw flexed. "I don't have any offensive devourer magic. Most magic doesn't work on me, but that's the extent of my devourer nature."

I grunted. "Then yes. My hammer is the only thing here that can actually kill them. Technically, they're not alive; that's why they'll recover from any mortal wound. The only way to take them out is to neutralize the dark magic powering them."

Twenty seconds, Viggo warned. *Coming from the south.*

Stay in the trees, I told him. Viggo was no match for a nidling. If I could have ordered Gunnar to run, I would have, but the wolf hated nidlings. He'd never leave.

"We could just fly away," Niall said tightly as we turned slightly to face the south.

"They won't stop tracking me." I shook my head. "They're fast and sneaky as hell. We can't risk them attacking us somewhere even more inconvenient and drawing the attention of the seraphim."

"What can I do to help you?" Niall pleaded, putting more distance between us so we each had room to work.

"They'll likely both target me. I need you to piss one of them off to draw it away from me." I swung the hammer a few times as adrenaline coursed through my body. "I got lucky with the first one; it gave me a solid opening. They usually don't go down that easy."

"Got it. I'm quite skilled at pissing things off."

"Shocking," I mumbled under my breath, most of my attention already on the dark woods, trusting Viggo to let me know if they changed direction.

Like two shadows peeling themselves off from the night, the nidlings entered the clearing. These were bigger than the first, easily six feet at the shoulder while they were on all fours. Solid white eyes glowed faintly, standing out against their pitch-black scales. Drool dripped from their misshapen jaws onto the forest floor.

My mind screamed, *WRONG!* Everything about them was an abomination. Dark magic had warped their bodies.

I was pretty sure they were originally some type of bear creature that had been forced to bond with the scale containing the essence of Nidhogg. Now they were nothing but a walking nightmare.

Both of them focused solely on me, paying no attention to Gunnar or Niall. Their bulky bodies should have made them slow and loud, but the magic that fueled their blood and muscles made them fast and silenced their movements.

It hit me then that I'd been leaving my blood all over this realm for the last few days from my sparring sessions with Niall. It should have occurred to me that Gullveig would use the nidlings to hunt me since they possessed the ability to slip between realms and had an uncanny sense of smell.

I'd definitely be berating myself later for this massive fuckup on my end.

"Try not to get bit," I warned. "The magic used to keep them going is potent, and if they do enough damage to your body, it will lead to an agonizing death."

The nidling on my left took a step closer, and I moved back, hoping to draw it away.

The one closer to me opened its mouth wider, a low-pitched voice tumbling out. "Siiiiigruuuuun."

"What the fuck?" Niall stared at the creature with a mix of horror and shock. The second one opened its mouth and echoed my name in the same whispering tone. "Oh, *fuck* this."

The fae warrior gracefully slid forward and sliced his dagger across the eye of the nidling closest to him. It snarled and shook its head but took another step towards me, other-wise unfazed.

Gunnar leapt onto its back and started tearing through the armor-like scales.

The nidling roared, and two things happened at once.

Niall took advantage of the exposed throat and slashed across it. And the other nidling lunged for me.

I spun out of the way and thrust the end of the hammer towards its eye, but I was too slow. The nidling's bulky head shied away, and the sharpened point bounced off the scales. A paw with three dagger-like claws dug into my side.

Pushing through the pain, I slammed my hammer down on the outstretched leg, right at the joint. Bone crunched as the nidling let out an agonizing snarl.

Instead of backing away, I swung the hammer again, aiming for the eye I had missed earlier. The nidling tried to sidestep my attack, but its leg gave out from underneath it. The orbital bone splintered beneath my blow, the eye destroyed and blood and liquids seeping out from the crushed socket.

I had less than a minute before the leg was fully healed. The eye would take longer, but not by much. It took an enormous amount of magic and power to make nidlings, but once they were created, the damn fuckers were near indestructible.

Curses and snarling told me that Gunnar and Niall were struggling to keep the other nidling distracted.

They had no doubt been given the order of finding me and bringing me to Gullveig. Their entire existence revolved around that task. Time was running out before the second nidling refocused its attention on me.

I hammered another hit to the eye I'd already damaged, then swung the weapon up to catch the underside of the beast's jaw, cutting off its growl.

With a quick practiced motion, I spun the hammer and started to thrust it upward, but the beast recovered too quickly and darted to the side, tucking its head back down to protect its vulnerable underside.

"Raise your fucking head!" I snarled.

Magic wound its way down the hammer's handle and nipped at me, wanting to be set free.

If I could pierce the nidling's flesh, it would take only a fraction of the weapon's power to neutralize it. The scales coating the beast were drenched with magic; cutting through them was difficult, and I'd have to let more of the hammer's magic go to beat through them.

"Sigrun!" Niall screamed a second before something slammed into my back and sent me flying towards the nidling I'd been facing off against.

I snapped my wings open, trying to change my course, but it was too late. Talons raked through my right wing, sending me spiraling to the ground. The nidling that had rammed me bit my arm on the way down, and I shrieked as both its teeth and magic tore into me.

The hammer tumbled from my grasp as I hit the earth, my blood seeping through the fallen leaves and pine needles.

Dark magic wound its way through my veins, setting my soul on fire.

I gasped and forced myself up on my hands and knees only to have another scream be torn out of me when claws raked down my back, pushing me further into the ground.

Sigrun! Viggo called out frantically.

Fine. Even in my mind, the word was slurred. *Stay.*

Suddenly, the nidling over me vanished, tearing out chunks of flesh and catching the edge of my wing as it left.

With a snarl, I shoved myself up, the hammer immediately leaping into my outstretched hand.

The nidling whose face I'd practically caved in earlier leapt for me, and I swung the hammer with both hands, putting all of my rage and strength into it. Agony tore through my damaged wing and back, but I shoved it down.

The beast crashed onto its side, and I was there in an instant, raising the hammer and bringing it down hard on its head.

Again. The beast struggled to rise. Again. Blood and gore splattered everywhere. Again.

It collapsed into a boneless heap, tremors running through

its body as the dark seidr magic powering it started piecing back together the head I'd smashed into nothing.

This time, when I raised the hammer, I flipped it and stabbed downward with the handle.

I released the stranglehold I kept over the hammer's magic, letting enough out to strike and burn through the magic of nidling. It stopped twitching as the smell of ozone became even heavier in the air.

Two down. One to go.

Gunnar's yelp tore through the clearing, and I immediately yanked the hammer free and ran towards him.

The remaining nidling had him pinned down with one paw and raised his other to tear the wolf's head off.

Niall was struggling to stand from where he'd been thrown halfway across the clearing; there was a wobble to his step as he shook his head. Blood poured from his forehead, painting half his face a dark red. We were both too far away to stop the nidling.

"No!" I screamed, throwing the hammer at the nidling's head even though I knew it would be too late.

A dark form dove out of the trees and yowled as it tore into the nidling's eyes. The paw crashed down towards Gunnar, but its aim was off, and the talons sunk into the ground next to the wolf's head.

The beast's head snapped to the side as my hammer slammed into it before immediately returning to my hand.

Niall was there in a flash, slashing his sword across the thick snout, forcing the nidling away from Gunnar. I hammered another hit to its head, with Niall striking immediately after. Neither of us relented, not giving the creature a second to recover. Viggo leapt off its head, and I was vaguely aware of him crouching in front of Gunnar's form, his low growl echoing through the forest.

In perfect unison, Niall and I beat the nidling back across

the clearing. My powerful strikes with the hammer keeping it unbalanced while his sword kept bleeding it dry. Even Nemain and I didn't fight this well together.

"The tree!" I shouted. "Pin it to the tree!"

I changed the angle of my hit, going for more of an upward strike against the nidling's skull. The moment my hit connected, the beast's head snapped up, and Niall thrust his sword through its neck, pinning it to the tree.

The nidling frantically tried to pull away, pulling its head down as much as possible in an attempt to protect its neck and soft underlying jaw.

Dark blood poured out of the wound where the sword had sliced through its flesh, and I slid to the side, shoving the handle of the hammer into its neck, right below Niall's blade where a few scales had been knocked loose.

The pointed end sunk in an inch and stopped. I threw my weight against it, and it gave another inch.

"Hurry," Niall grunted as he kept pressure on the sword even as the nidling tore into his side with its claws.

I leaned back before flinging all of my weight forward, and the scales finally gave way. With one thought from me, magic pulsed from the hammer, and nidling sagged against the tree as its body slowly crumbled into nothing.

Niall grimaced as he wrapped a hand around his ribs. "You have some seriously fucked-up enemies, álainn."

"I'm aware." I rasped as a sharp pain wracked my sides. Gritting my teeth, I forced my body to move through the pain and raced to where Viggo was crouched next to Gunnar.

The wolf's white coat was soaked with blood, and panic ripped through me until I saw the rise and fall of his breaths. He struggled to rise as I knelt by him, and I had to gently push him back to the ground.

"Easy, my friend," I urged, though I let out a breath of relief that he still lived. That had been too close.

Viggo crouched on the other side of the wolf, his tail flipping back and forth nervously. I sensed Niall approaching behind me.

"Get my bag," I ordered roughly. "I need to help him heal."

The source of the blood seemed to be from two deep gouges along his sides where the nidling had attempted to cut him with its claws.

Ever so carefully, I ran my fingers through his fur, checking for bites. Healing those was outside of my ability, but I could speed along the rest of the healing. Viggo was uncharacteristically quiet as he waited by Gunnar's head, one paw outstretched to gently rest on the wolf's muzzle.

"I can heal him," Niall said softly. He stood next to me, holding my bag.

My dark eyes met his bright ones. "Are you sure?"

A soft whimper escaped Gunnar when my fingers found another wound beneath the matted fur and blood. Thankfully, all the wounds so far had been from talons, not teeth. Niall might be able to heal the physical injuries, but I doubted he could handle the dark magic left behind from a nidling bite.

"Yes," Niall said before looking over my broken wing and the blood dripping down my side. "Maybe I should heal you first, though. I'm not a particularly gifted healer. I can only heal one of you now, then I'll need to wait for my magic to recover before doing the other."

"Him first," I said without any hesitation. "I'll be fine."

Lie. I was anything but fine. But my body would eventually heal most of the wounds, and I could push through the pain.

Gunnar had no innate healing abilities.

I had to give him credit, Niall only hesitated for a moment before gently laying his hands on the wolf's side. Gunnar flinched at the contact of a stranger on him but held still as Viggo rubbed the side of his face against his.

"Sorry," Niall murmured. "I'm not the most elegant of healers, and I require contact to use my magic on others."

Seconds ticked by while I stared at the bloody wounds, as if my will for Gunnar to be okay would speed up the fae's magic. Finally, the flow of blood slowed. The fur was too thick for me to see his injuries without moving it aside, but I assumed Niall's magic was working.

After a minute, he pulled his hands away and settled back on his haunches with a deep sigh.

A quick check of Gunnar's side revealed all the skin had closed back up, and I let out a relieved breath.

He'd been wounded in fights before, and every time I was terrified I would lose him. But he was a wolf, and I would never order him to defy his nature. Even if it cost him his life one day.

"Come on, wolf," I urged. "Get up so I can check your other side."

Viggo shifted back, allowing Gunnar room to stand up, which he did so slower than normal and without his usual lupine grace. A quick perusal told me he didn't have any significant injuries on that side, only a few minor cuts.

"He'll probably be sore," Niall said tiredly, his face drawn and pale from exertion. "But I healed the internal damage. There was… a lot."

"Thank you," I breathed. "I don't know what I would have done if I had lost him."

Even though I knew he was okay, my body still hadn't caught up to that fact yet. I stared down at my fingers that were still trembling slightly and covered in blood.

Niall got up and returned moments later with a container of water and some cloth. He sprinkled water over my hands and forearms, his fingers rubbing away the worst of the blood and grime as he slowly poured more water over them to rinse everything off.

Neither of us spoke as he worked to clean me up. I couldn't remember the last time someone had taken care of me after a fight.

"What does *álainn* mean?" The words came out a little breathy, and I cleared my throat. "You called me that earlier, and my translation mark didn't recognize it."

Niall's lips curled up in a smile, but he didn't answer right away, instead, he just continued to clean my hands and arms. Once he was satisfied, he grabbed the remaining cloth and dampened it with some water before leaning forward and gently wiping my face.

I held perfectly still while he worked, but when his thumb brushed across my bottom lip, even my heart seemed to go still.

"Beautiful one," he said softly. "It means beautiful one in sciatháin."

Niall's focus was on my lips as he slowly dragged his finger across them again before raising his eyes to meet mine.

My heart that had been so still a moment ago suddenly started beating rapidly. At first, I'd been able to dismiss my feelings towards Niall as lust. It was a natural reaction, one that I'd been able to identify, acknowledge, and then lock away in a box.

But what I was feeling now… this was so much more than that.

Every time he touched me, it felt like he was leaving behind a trail of heat on my skin.

My body was rapidly beginning to crave every single one of those touches no matter how light or innocent they may prove to be.

And what's more, I enjoyed every time I said something to get a smile out of him. His deep laughs made my soul feel lighter no matter what dark thought I was dwelling on. I enjoyed having Niall near, and the thought of separating from him sent a pulse of anxiety straight through me.

And that was a problem. Niall wasn't mine to claim. I'd only known him for a few days, and up until recently he'd been working for our enemy.

It was foolish of me to allow myself to feel this way. I needed to be careful and put some distance between us.

"We should move," I said in a rough voice before I forced myself to my feet.

Pain laced up my side and down my back, and a hiss of pain slid from my lips. Definitely cracked some ribs in that fight. They'd heal fast, but it'd still hurt to breathe for the next hour. My wing would take a lot longer to heal.

Once we were somewhere safe, I'd make a healing tea to help move things along. The bite on my arm was the bigger concern. It meant there was a ticking clock on how much time I had left to finish things up here and find a healer.

I cleared my throat, my focus returning to the matter at hand. "That fight was loud, and the seraphim might send some scouts out to investigate."

Niall nodded. "The bodies have mostly fallen apart; we can scatter the remains. But we should take a few minutes to break apart the firewood and hide our footprints."

He started walking towards the fire, limping a little on his left leg. I whispered some words under my breath and he halted, spinning back around to face me even as his eyes darted around the clearing.

"You even hid the footprints… I'm impressed, álainn."

"You shouldn't call me that." I gave him my best hard stare.

"Ah, but it's so fitting." He grinned unrepentantly. "I find myself unable to call you anything else."

My mouth flattened into a hard line, which only caused him to grin wider. "You're impossible," I muttered. "Like I said before, no one can surpass the illusion magic of those from Yggdrasil."

Niall accepted this and returned his attention to the forest floor as he scanned the area again. "How long will it last?"

"Long enough." I started to shrug but killed the motion when the movement invoked a jolt of pain from my injured wing. Technically, I could make it last until someone broke the spell, but there was no need to dump that much magic into it. The seraphim would be moving on from this area come morning.

Gripping the bag to my chest, as there was no way I could carry it on my back, I set off into the forest.

I didn't want to go too far away from the seraphim camp, so I took a diagonal path that put distance between us and where we'd been camping but didn't add much between us and the seraphim.

Gunnar was already gaining back some of his lupine grace and scouted ahead of us, but he kept close enough that he remained within sight. Viggo once again took to the top of the tree canopy so that he could keep an eye out for seraphim soldiers.

It didn't take long before he called out a warning.

Three seraph scouts incoming, he said. *Looks like they're just doing a standard sweep. I don't think they're specifically coming for us.*

I let out a low whistle, and Gunnar immediately returned to my side. My fingers dug into his fur, and I stretched a hand out to Niall.

His eyes flicked back and forth between my face and hand before he slid his fingers into mine.

Given that he was a devourer, this probably wouldn't work, but I figured it was worth a shot. The trees weren't as thick in this area, and we'd be easy to spot from the sky.

Magic slipped out from me. The illusion spell was one of the few that didn't require me to speak any words or use herbs to channel.

It coated me and Gunnar in an instant, but when it reached Niall, it sank into him.

My brows furrowed, my will raising more power.

More of my magic poured out of me and directly into him. Panic thrummed in my chest as I felt my magic slip away. We both pulled our hands apart at the same time.

"Sorry." He shifted slightly. "I thought maybe because your magic is so different from anything I've encountered before that it might work. Are you okay?"

"Fine," I rasped out. My body was already feeling over-taxed from healing, and now fatigue threatened to pull me under. "You need to hide yourself."

He nodded and retreated further into the underbrush, then extended his black wings over his form. It wasn't perfect; a black blob tended to stand out. Luckily, it was an overcast night, and the seraphim couldn't see that well in the dark.

Once I felt my magic coat my skin again, I knelt down next to Gunnar before my legs completely gave out.

I should have known better than to try and use my magic on him. It was just odd interacting with a devourer who wasn't a raving beast. Technically, Nemain and Kalen were devourer hybrids, but they were born that way, not made. Different rules applied to them, and it was easy to forget sometimes what they were.

With an unsettling realization, it occurred to me that Niall was now in that category too. When I looked at him, I didn't see a devourer. I barely even registered him as fae. He was just... Niall. It wasn't like me to be this trusting of someone so soon, but he was easily sliding past all my defenses, and I didn't know how to stop him. Or if I even wanted to stop him.

The minutes ticked by, but soon three silhouettes glided overhead. One broke off from the other two and circled a few times, flying low enough to clip the tree line.

We all held still, even after they left, until Viggo gave the all-clear.

"Let's go a little further and find a place where the trees are denser to rest for what remains of the night." A pained grunt spilled out of me before I could bite it back as soon as the words left my mouth.

Niall was there in an instant, a concerned and slightly guilty look on his face as his eyes took in my still-healing wounds.

"I'm fine," I insisted, unable to hide the edge to my voice. It was my choice to heal Gunnar first, and I didn't regret it.

"You're not." He shook his head. "It's my fault. When you tried to hide me earlier, I took some of your magic. I didn't mean to, but I can't control it. The devourer part of me instantly absorbs any magic thrown at it, even if that magic is well-intentioned."

"Would have been nice to know that earlier."

"Like I said,"—he gave me an apologetic shrug—"I thought it might work."

"I can make it a little bit further." I tried to step around him, but he mirrored my movement.

"At least let me heal your wing and ribs. I got a boost from the magic I took from you, so I'm good to do a little more healing now. We'll deal with your arm later."

I glared at him, but the resolve in his face didn't budge. Fine. With a sigh, I dropped my bag and raised my arm, allowing him access to my ribs.

He stepped closer until I could feel the heat radiating off him and gently placed a hand on my side. Despite my injuries, a contented sigh slipped from my lips at the contact. Niall's hand stilled.

"Sorry," he whispered. "I didn't mean to hurt you."

"You didn't." I didn't offer any other explanation.

His lips quirked up into a smile, and I didn't realize I was staring at them until his smile broadened even more. "Better?"

Exhaustion and pain. That's why I'd been staring at him. It had to be. I was too old for this nonsense.

"Yes." I jerked my head in a nod and stepped away. His hand trailed across my side before he let it drop, and I instantly missed the contact.

"Now your wing." He shifted to the side so he could get a better look and grimaced. "I'm going to have to hold it up with one hand so that the bones heal correctly. Tell me when you're ready."

I spread my feet a litter further apart and then picked a patch of moss growing on one of the trees in front of me to focus on. "Ready."

Niall's movements were smooth and quick, but there were multiple broken bones and torn ligaments in my wing. Not to mention the deep gouges down my back.

"Fuck!" I ground out after swallowing the scream that tried to burst out of my chest.

By the time he got my wing into position, I was panting heavily, but my eyes never waved from the moss.

I couldn't afford to blackout now. Niall might be a temporary ally of sorts, but I couldn't afford to trust him completely. My instincts were also telling me that he was hiding something, which meant I needed to be wary around him until I figured out what it was.

Then again... who wouldn't have secrets after thousands of years of living?

After what felt like hours but was probably less than ten minutes, Niall finally released my wing and stepped back. I turned around to face him and barely had time to catch him when he stumbled forward. His large hands gripped my shoulders as I supported most of his weight.

"What's wrong?" I asked urgently.

Trembles racked his frame as he leaned harder into me.

"Don't know," he mumbled. "For some reason, that was a lot harder than it should have been. Like your magic was fighting me."

Shit. *My* magic wasn't the problem; it was the dark magic seeping further into me thanks to the nidling bite on my arm.

Now that the pain from my wing and ribs was gone, I could feel how numb my arm was. It'd already spread further up, almost to my shoulder, which meant I had less time that I thought.

"Lean on me," I told him. "We'll go just a little bit further, and then I'll keep watch while you rest."

He grunted but didn't protest as I wrapped an arm around his waist.

"I was really hoping this would go the other way," he said tiredly. "That maybe you'd swoon after I healed you, and I could carry you off to safety."

I snorted even as a smile tugged at my lips. "You're kind of ridiculous. You know that, right?"

"I'll be whatever it takes to make you happy, álainn."

Chapter Seven

I SENSED her presence only a second before a fine mist rolled across the small clearing where we'd bedded down for the night.

Niall had instantly passed out as soon as he'd leaned against a tree. Surprisingly, Gunnar had fallen asleep at his side, with his head resting on the fae's thigh. Viggo was snuggled up on the wolf's other side.

My body desperately wanted sleep, but I had forced myself to stay awake.

I would only grow weaker as the magic from the nidling bite spread. Sleep wouldn't help me, but it would help the others, so I let them have it while I stood watch.

If it had been a normal mist, I was sure they would have awoken instantly when the seraph landed mere feet from where we rested. But the magic within the mist nipped at my skin as it rolled over me.

I was on my feet with the hammer in my hands before the seraph even finished pulling their wings back.

Her current body belonged to a strong male seraph, probably in his prime based on his well-muscled physique and the scars across his body that declared he'd seen battle many times over yet always emerged victorious.

But the eyes... those were not his eyes. The pale milky white eyes were clouded, as if a film was over them. Somehow seeing nothing and everything at once.

"Gullveig," I said flatly as I moved to stand between her and my sleeping companions. "Expending an awful lot of magic to come and check up on little old me."

"I couldn't resist," a feminine voice said from the lips of the seraph. "You've been hard to track down lately, and when my hounds got a taste of your flesh..." The seraph smacked his lips in a way that was purely Gullveig, and it made my stomach turn. "How's the bite, by the way? Do you feel it crawling through your body?"

The seraph's head cocked to the side and inhaled deeply.

"Ooooh. It got you real good. The seraphim realm isn't a good place for a valkyrie to be weakened. Perhaps you should come and pay me a visit. I could fix you right up."

I fixed my face into a mask of indifference and fought against the trembling in my spine from holding myself upright. She was right, the magic from the bite was spreading quickly. In my current state, I was no match for Gullveig; she'd overpower me easily and then claim what she always wanted.

The hammer... and my power. I couldn't let that happen.

"Funny, I've been trying to stop by for a visit for months now," I said primly. "But you haven't responded to any of my requests."

The seraph's head snapped back and then to the side again, their eyes flashing a dark green for a second before fading back to white.

"Control problems?" I drawled, spinning the hammer around in my hand. "I have a fix for that."

The seraph shrugged, the movement jerky and unnatural. "These creatures aren't the brightest, but they have strong wills. And their power…" The seraph raised their hands to the side, and bright orange flames sprung into existence. "Their power is downright *delicious*. Even after expending some energy to fling my soul to this godsforsaken realm and take up residence in this brute, I'm going to be sated and sleep well tonight."

"Let's hear it." My lip curled in distaste.

This entire clearing was now tainted with Gullveig's particular brand of dark magic, and the wrongness of it all was making my skin crawl.

The seraph gave me a close-lipped smile as Gullveig twisted the body around to get a better look at Niall. I instantly snapped my wings open, blocking her view, and a husky laugh filled the forest despite the seraph's mouth remaining closed.

The hairs on the back of my neck stood on end, but I kept my expression neutral.

"You're here to offer me a deal. Let's hear it," I said again.

It was the only reason I hadn't smashed the seraph's head in the moment it landed in the clearing. Gullveig had gone to a lot of trouble to chat with me tonight, and I wanted to know why.

"Surrender yourself to me"—the seraph's white eyes latched onto the hammer—"with the hammer, and I will swear to leave your shiny new valkyrie apprentice alone. And all your newfound friends. I'll even be generous and throw in that runt of a feline and the self-righteous wolf."

Gullveig was a lot of things, but a liar wasn't one of them. Still… I knew she wanted Bryn.

I was currently the most powerful valkyrie in existence, but Bryn had the potential to surpass me one day. Gullveig was well aware of how I'd come into my power and what the hammer truly contained.

She would try to recreate it using Bryn and Finn. It didn't make any sense for her to give that opportunity up. Unless…

"You've seen something," I guessed, and the seraph went completely still. "Something that has you worried enough to make this offer. What did you see?"

After the events of Ragnarok, most of those with the seer gift had been exterminated throughout the Yggdrasil realms. But Gullveig had already gone into hiding at that point. I didn't know how strong her gift of prophecy was, but I suspected it rivaled that of the fae.

The seraph didn't move an inch while Gullveig pondered me through his eyes before finally answering my question. "It doesn't matter what path the boy chooses. Light or dark. He will bring chaos to all our worlds."

"Prophecies have been wrong before," I said tightly.

After all the prophecy bullshit around Ragnarok, it turned out to be nothing more than a self-fulfilling prophecy that fractured our realms. So much life had been lost for nothing. I didn't agree with the slaughter that took place against those with seer lines, but I understood why the Valkyrie Queen had taken that action.

"I am not wrong." The seraphim's expression took on a hungry edge. "Personally, I'm looking forward to the chaos that he will unleash. But I want to be prepared for that day. Hence my offer."

"No," I said evenly. "I will never again let prophecy dictate my future."

"Sigrun," she crooned, tilting the seraph's head, "do you really want to go through another war? Because that's what's coming. After everything you went through in the last one… aren't you tired?"

I couldn't deny the truth of her words. In the years after Ragnarok, my soul had been so fucking exhausted. There were days when I couldn't get out of bed.

When the valkyries and others had come for me, I'd barely put up a fight. But no matter how many times my body was torn apart, I always came back. And slowly, I started to piece my soul back together, too.

Gunnar and Viggo helped. Then Nemain. And now I had Bryn.

"My answer remains the same." I raised my chin and let her see the resolve in my eyes. "I'm coming for you, Gullveig. And once I'm done with you, I will help my friends in whatever comes for us. If it's a war, then so be it."

"We'll see." The seraph's cloudy eyes latched onto the wound on my arm. "I'll ask you again soon, when you've had more time to consider my offer."

The mist rolling through the clearing started to retreat as the true color of the seraph's eyes bled through the cloudy white once more. The seraph staggered forward before collapsing to his knees as Gullveig left his body and stole his vitality.

He clutched his chest as dark veins appeared across his skin and fell against the forest floor.

"Valkyrie," he gasped. "End… this…"

I lowered my hammer until it rested on his chest right above his heart. A bolt of magic shot out, and the seraph lay still, one final breath leaking from his lips.

I hated the seraphim with every fiber of my being.

But that didn't stop me from leaning down and gently brushing his eyes closed.

It took us a little over two days to reach the sprawling city Niall had seen upon first arriving in the seraphim realm.

Gullveig hadn't paid me anymore visits, not that I really expected her to. She'd said her piece, and I'd given her my answer. All that was left for us now was to have our final face-off. Niall had fully recovered, but I was only getting worse thanks to the damn nidling bite.

"How's the arm?" Niall scrutinized the bandages I'd wrapped around my forearm and reached out to inspect it.

"Fine," I said tightly, pulling away from his reach.

In addition to the bandages, I'd also cast an illusion spell over it to hide the dark magic. But using magic to hide other magic was tricky, and I wasn't sure it would hold up to close examination.

Niall had been pissy the last two days because I'd refused to let him look at it and try to heal the wound again. It wouldn't work, and it'd only end up hurting him.

I was glad we had reached the city when we did because I was pretty sure Niall was thinking about tackling me and holding me down while he inspected my arm. The way Gunnar and Viggo were hovering around me at all times made me think that they would help him.

The dense forest that covered this region had been cut back quite a ways from the city. There were two perimeter walls, one around the main part of the city, and then an outer ring where crops and livestock were held.

And likely humans, although I hadn't spotted any from my quick preliminary fly-over. If they had humans penned up here like the other cities, they must be holding them in the back half.

Aside from its enormous size, the city looked the same as all the others. The buildings and perimeter wall were all made of the same limestone-like material and shone a bright white in the morning sun. The glare unsettled me and made it hard to stare at the city for long, as the buildings tended to blur together, and any architectural differences were lost in the sea of white bricks and walls.

It's like bleach straight to your eyeballs. Viggo scrunched his nose up in distaste.

"It really is," I agreed. "Their eyesight must function differently than ours because it's downright painful to stare at for more than a few seconds."

"I think we should reevaluate the plan," Niall said in the same tight tone he'd been using all day.

"You've been saying that for two days." I cut him an annoyed look. "Viggo and I have the best chance of scouting around the city. We won't take any more risks than we need to. If we don't find anything, we'll just leave."

Niall clenched his jaw but jerked his head in agreement. There was no way for him to move around in the city undetected, and we'd already established my magic didn't work on him.

I'd debated sending Viggo in on his own, since his smaller form made it easier for him to navigate, but I didn't want to risk him being discovered by Lir. Especially with the memory of almost losing Gunnar still so sharp and vivid in my mind. Viggo was skilled at being hidden but he could also be reckless sometimes. I'd just have to hope the city wasn't too crowded inside and that no one bumped into me.

As if sensing the turmoil of my thoughts, Gunnar leaned against my leg, and I gave him a good scratch behind his ears.

I murmured, "If you need to retreat, head west and I'll find you."

The wolf let out a soft woof before trotting off and settling down between two trees at the edge of the tree line. Wordlessly, Niall followed after him, his posture still stiff.

"Ready?" I asked Viggo.

Of course. A shimmer fell over his fluffy brown coat and he leapt into the air, bounding towards the city.

I donned my own invisibility spell and took off into the air as well. My wing and back still felt tight, and there was a slight ache, as if I'd just had a strenuous workout.

But without Niall's healing, it would have taken a lot longer to recover.

Let's stick together as much as possible, I pushed the thought past my mental defenses.

Valkyries weren't particularly gifted telepaths; we could only communicate with beings who had strong telepathic abilities like Viggo. But our ability to block any type of telepathic attack was strong. Even the most powerful telepaths would have trouble breaching our inner walls.

Gullveig could do it, but only in conjunction with seidr magic. If you were able to disrupt the magic, then she didn't stand a chance.

I'd encountered a few telepaths who were capable of breaking into my mind over the course of my long life, and I'd killed all of them except one.

Isabeau.

Nemain's young vampire ward was packing some intense mental-based magic. During her first encounter with Viggo, she's scared the hell out of the skoggkat. It had taken me a while to get the truth out of him, but he eventually told me.

The little girl had trapped him in his own mind, on a loop of the day his mother and siblings had been killed.

She'd launched the attack in seconds and had not only torn through his mental shields but had also dived deep into his mind and found the most traumatic memory, using it against him.

He refused to be in the same room with her now and called her a monster.

I didn't disagree.

But Nemain was fiercely protective of Isabeau, as was the fae boy, Finn. I hadn't told anyone yet what she'd done to Viggo, but I needed to soon.

If she was already this powerful, who knew what she would be capable of in a decade? But I had to tread carefully. Isabeau was surrounded by people who wielded all sorts of dark and fucked-up magic.

They were all monsters, but they protected their own.

Given the hammer I carried on my back and what the valkyries thought of me, I supposed I was a monster too.

We'll cover more ground if we split up, Viggo argued.

He leapt through the air nimbly, keeping pace with me as I flapped my wings.

I'd carried him on our flight here, which he hadn't been rather happy about, but I could fly a lot faster than he could maneuver through the air. Despite my constant reassurance, Viggo always felt like he had something to prove. It often made him brash, which was why he was an endless concern for me and Gunnar.

I'm not sure what these fae devourers are capable of. I alternated our direction towards a tall building in the center of the city. *Niall can't see us while we're cloaked, but I know Lir is sidhe, and I'm pretty sure most of the fae he travels around with are as well. Before we get too hasty, we should confirm that they can't see us.*

Regular sidhe can't see us, Viggo scoffed. *No reason these devourer freaks would be able to.*

I let out a frustrated sigh. *For once, Viggo, don't argue with me.*

Fine, he said sulkily.

We landed without incident on a rooftop balcony and perched on the wall to survey the city.

This one was similar to all the other ones we'd infiltrated, it was just much—much bigger. Most cities had populations between ten and twenty thousand seraphim. Based on how far this city sprawled and how dense the buildings were, this one housed at least a hundred thousand.

If the possibility of learning some of Lir's secrets wasn't on the line, I absolutely would not have chanced going in. Viggo and I would have to be extra careful to remain undetected.

I watched the seraph guards soar around the city. Despite my hatred of the seraphim, I had to give them credit for how well they organized their armies and guarded their cities.

They knew that it was only a matter of time until the fae or daemons caught wind of what they were doing and invaded this realm, so they prepared, and they did it well. They treated every single day like it would be the one when the invasion happened.

Part of me wanted to go to the Valkyrie Queen and tell her what was going on. The seraphim were our enemy, and we never allowed our enemies to grow this powerful in the past.

But my words of caution would likely fall on deaf ears.

The last time I'd tried to enter the valkyrie stronghold, they'd attempted to cut my wings off and spent the next decade hunting me across the realms.

There, Viggo said, leaping from the roof before I could stop him.

I killed the growl that rose up my throat and silently flew after him. He nimbly traveled through the air, keeping low enough to avoid the seraphs that flew above the city. Luckily, most of them seemed content to walk, so the skies weren't too congested.

Viggo landed on one of the few two-story buildings in this part of the city. It made up for its short height by having a sprawling roof deck full of chairs and tables. Seraphs lounged around in varying stages of inebriation despite it not even being lunch time yet. Likely off-duty soldiers. Most seraphim had two modes: disciplined and bloodthirsty soldier or inebriated, drunk asshole.

One of them leaned over the railing and hurled before falling over with a yelp and landing with a hard thud.

His drinking buddies peered over the railing and then threw their heads back, bellowing in laughter. I grimaced and pulled my wings tighter to myself, edging closer to the corner that was currently empty where Viggo was perched.

Directly across from us was a six-story building. Guards were posted at the entrance, and I spotted more lining the roof.

Large archways on each floor gave us a clear view into the building, and on the second floor was a group of sidhe warriors. Even from here I could feel the wrongness of their magic, the taint of devourer.

I'd gotten used to it around Niall, but his devourer magic was like a candle compared to the bonfire of these sidhe.

All of them were gathered around a large table with a map spread out across it. A towering sidhe male with pale skin and steel grey hair was pointing at something in the corner, and they were all focusing on that.

Lir. It had to be. I couldn't see if he had light blue eyes from here, but he matched the description that Nemain had provided.

Do a quick pass in front of the windows, I told Viggo. *I'll watch for any reaction from them.*

The skogkatt took off immediately and zigzagged in front of the windows several times before joining me again. None of the sidhe raised their heads or gave any indication that they had seen anything.

Alright, let's get closer so we can hear them. But be ready to hightail it out of here if I say so.

I turned on my heels, angling my body towards the center window, when a pain shot through my shoulder and spread down my chest.

A deep hiss slipped from my lips before I could crush it. My heart rate shot up, and I looked around to see if anyone had heard me, but thankfully all the seraphim on the rooftop were too drunk, and the ones guarding the building across from us were too far away.

Sigrun? Viggo inquired. *What's wrong?*

Arm. Even in my mind, the word felt heavy, my thoughts growing sluggish. *Spreading.*

Uncertainly flashed in his eyes. Viggo had no doubt known

something was wrong with my arm, but he'd never fought nidlings before.

In his eyes, I was damn near invincible. And to some degree, I was. I couldn't die. No matter what was done to my body, it would eventually regenerate, and my soul would hover over it until it could slip back inside.

But there were far worse things than death, and I unfortunately was familiar with quite a few of them.

Do we need to head back? he asked, shifting nervously from paw to paw.

No. Not yet. I squeezed my eyes shut and concentrated on my breathing. The dark magic was creeping closer to my heart and lungs. Once it reached those, I was in serious trouble.

Moving would be out of the question, as the pain from breathing alone would knock me on my ass. It wouldn't kill me, but the pain would only increase until I found someone who could undo the magic. I concentrated on feeling where the magic was and then quickly calculated how long it had taken to spread.

An hour. I should have an hour, maybe a little less. The pain would continue to amp up, but I refused to waste this opportunity.

Thirty minutes, I said. *We'll gather whatever information we can for thirty minutes, and then we'll head back.*

Viggo looked at me doubtfully but for once didn't argue. I clenched my jaw and made the short flight to one of the arched openings, uneasily perching inside it. Sweat poured out of me as the pain increased, but I remained in the window like a statue, listening to the general of Balor's army discuss plans with several seraph generals.

No doubt we could have learned more if we stayed for more than thirty minutes. But even then, we picked up all kinds of useful information, including one glaring fact.

The human realm was totally fucked.

Chapter Eight

As much as I'd wanted to stay and keep listening, I'd already collected a lot of vital information, and I needed to get it to Nemain or Pele as soon as possible.

Every breath felt like inhaling glass shards, and my vision was growing dark around the edges by the second. I'd pushed it too far, and now there was a very real chance I wouldn't make it back to Gunnar and Niall.

My jump from the archway was more of a tumble, but I managed to beat my wings enough to carry me up and over the buildings. Viggo kept pace beside me, providing me words of encouragement as we flew across the city. Relief flooded me when we passed over the perimeter wall, but the momentary loss of focus cost me.

Pain racked up my back, and my wings froze mid-stroke. The world swirled and darkened around me as I fell from the sky and slammed into the earth.

If I'd been capable of screaming, my arm snapping in at least two places definitely would have done it.

Instead, all I could do was wheeze and cough up some blood.

Sigrun! I felt Viggo's soft fur brush against my face. *You have to get up! We flew in the wrong direction. Gunnar and that fae prick are on the other side.*

Can't. The word was barely a whisper in my mind, and I had no idea if Viggo heard me or not.

The dark magic had spread too far, and my body was lost to me, but I fought to keep the invisibility spell in place. We were still close enough to the wall that the seraph guards would easily spot me, and I didn't stand a chance in a fight in my current state.

My broken arm was pinned beneath me, and I tried not to jostle it as I slowly reached into the slim pouch attached to my belt and pulled out a small purple crystal.

"Get. Others," I breathed, too far gone to try and lower my mental shields to communicate telepathically any longer.

Viggo took off like a shot and I clenched the crystal, sending my will into it. The spell it contained was crafted by a daemon, a fact I was really thankful for at the moment.

If it'd been the fae who had created the summoning crystal, it no doubt would have been prettier but probably would have required something more intricate than merely shoving my will into it. Maybe a whispered poetic word or elaborately tracing a pattern across its smooth surface.

The fae made everything beautiful. The daemons made it functional.

As much as I hated the idea of giving Nemain something to lord over me with, and she would absolutely mock me about saving me from the godsdamned angels because of one lousy bite, I'd really been counting on her immediately showing up.

But my hope started to dwindle as the minutes ticked by and no gateway opened. Was she still in the dragon realm? It had been weeks. Had something gone wrong?

Even concern for my friend couldn't keep me conscious. I

blacked out several times only for excruciating pain to jolt me awake again.

Seraph guards were perched on the perimeter walls; I'd made it outside of the city but just barely. The invisibility spell was easy to cast, but it did require a constant trickle of magic, and I was using the last of my abilities to not only hide myself but also Gunnar. The seraphim would no doubt be on the lookout for a winged white wolf after our attack on the city weeks ago. Every time I blacked out, I risked cutting off the flow of magic and exposing us both.

My gold wings would be a beacon to the seraphim. They would rip me apart and devour my flesh. I'd died many times before, but my body always regenerated. I wasn't sure what would happen if I was eaten, though.

Would my soul be cursed to wander the realms for eternity? Or would Hel finally claim me?

Valhalla would never welcome me.

When my vision started to darken again, I clung to consciousness. Every beat of my heart sent a fresh wave of agony through my body, and I dreaded every breath for the fire it poured into my lungs.

"Hurry, Viggo." My words served as more a prayer than anything else.

After what felt like an eternity, Gunnar appeared above me. He lowered his head and gently nuzzled my cheek with a soft whine.

Viggo came into view as well, his gaze on the crystal in my hand. His eyes rose to meet mine, and I knew he understood. Help wasn't coming.

We need to get you away from the city before you lose control of your magic. That idiot fae you let tag along is in the woods behind us, but he can't help to move you without being spotted.

"Gunnar will have to drag me," I said before using the last of my strength to flip over onto my stomach so that my wings wouldn't get damaged anymore, offering Gunnar a place to grab hold of.

This will hurt, Viggo warned.

I gritted my teeth and gave them a tight nod of acknowledgement.

As always, Gunnar understood what I needed from him. He maneuvered around me and carefully grabbed the leather harness that strapped the hammer to my back.

Despite his efforts to move quickly but smoothly, there was nothing that could be done about the mind-splitting pain that erupted from my broken body at being dragged across the ground. I wanted to embrace the darkness and let myself pass out, but I knew that if I did, my spell would falter and the seraphim would see us.

Viggo and Gunnar would fight to the death for me. I refused to lose them, so I pushed back with everything I had against the sweet, tempting calls of the dark.

It wasn't enough.

The ground grew rougher. Rock that had been exposed to the elements poked out from the earth.

Gunnar tried his best to avoid them, but he was walking backwards and concentrating on keeping the pace steady. Something sharp and rough cut against skin and pulled on my broken arm.

A scream tore out of me, and then I saw nothing.

Familiar green eyes peered at me from a face that was also familiar... but not. I tried to sit up, but my body informed me very quickly that was a bad idea.

Also probably not physically possible.

"Badb," I croaked, "what happened?"

"I was hoping you could tell me." The feline shifter known

to most as The Morrigan leaned back in the chair she was sitting in as she studied me.

Like her daughter, she favored simple but functional black clothes and wore her ashen blonde hair in a thick braid that rested over her shoulder. Nemain may have her father to thank for her dark and twisted magic, but she was the spitting image of Badb.

"A few hours ago, I was dropping something off in Nemain's apartment when I noticed the summoning crystal in her living room glowing bright enough to blind anyone who looked at it too long."

What? My brow furrowed together as I tried to understand. I'd been holding onto the crystal, and I'd activated it, which would have lit up the crystal that Nemain kept in her apartment, letting her know I was ready for a gateway to be opened. I'd seen the crystals in action before; they just gave off a faint glow when active.

"Ah." Badb pursed her lips. "You didn't know."

"Know…" I licked my lips. "What?"

Badb raised her gaze to the ceiling, her pretty features tight with frustration.

"The summoning crystals only take a few seconds to activate. Once they've received the command, they can be released. The pair will continue to glow faintly until the person with the second crystal clears the command. But if the person with the summoning crystal holds onto it for longer than thirty seconds and continues to activate, the second crystal will glow brightly.

"The longer the hold, the brighter the light. Given that the thing was as bright as the damn sun, you must have been holding onto it for at least an hour before I got there."

"Oh." My head thumped back against the soft pillow. "That would have been good to know."

"Nemain has had a lot on her mind lately," Badb sighed. "She must have forgotten."

Slowly, I pushed myself up to a sitting position. As I suspected, I was on a bed. But I didn't recognize the room at all. This wasn't Nemain's apartment, but the furnishings looked like standard human stuff. Where the hell was I?

I also felt a little better. My mind felt like it'd been deprived of sleep for weeks, and my body felt like it'd gone through a meat grinder. But it was better than the debilitating pain I'd felt in the seraphim realm. I glanced down at my arm and saw that it had been wrapped with a fresh bandage.

Unfortunately, the invisibility cloak I'd cast over it had vanished when I lost consciousness. Where the bandage ended, black veins spread beneath my skin.

"What the hell is going on?" I wasn't exactly sure whether I should address the shifter as Morrigan or Badb. The former was her title, while the second was her name. I didn't know her well enough to know what she preferred or what was proper.

Despite not being fae, she was a high-ranking member of the Unseelie Court. Most of the court was comprised of the sidhe, and they loved their titles. Nemain's mother struck me as the type of person who didn't give a shit.

But then again, she also seemed like the type to wield her title as The Morrigan as a weapon.

She passed me a glass of water, and I greedily drank it down. My eyes darted around the room, and I relaxed slightly when I saw Gunnar and Viggo curled up in the corner. The skogkatt was fast asleep, but Gunnar's crystal-blue eyes were on me.

I smiled at him so he knew I was okay, and he tucked his head between his paws and closed his eyes.

"Nemain is busy dealing with the dragons she brought back from the dragon realm with her. You're lucky that I stopped by her apartment when I did."

"I am." I nodded in acknowledgement.

"Imagine my surprise when I opened a gateway to find you passed out with your two furballs guarding you furiously while a strange fae male fought off droves of seraphim."

Shit. Niall.

"Is he okay?" I asked quickly.

Badb stared at me, a deranged smile spreading across her lips. "The last time I saw that fae prick, I told him that if we ever crossed paths again, I'd kill him."

"Badb—" I jolted upright and sucked in a harsh breath as pain struck my chest at the sudden movement, but it was nothing compared to the agony of thinking I'd lost Niall.

"Relax." She waved her hand dismissively. "I didn't kill him. *Yet.*"

It took several seconds for my heart to stop racing, and I slowly lowered myself back down. Her words didn't entirely ease my tension because her tone made it very clear that Niall's life was still on the line.

I had no illusions about Badb because I had heard every rumor and story about The Morrigan and her mate, The Erlking. The two of them were killers, and while I wouldn't consider them evil the way I did Gullveig, whatever morals they possessed were far darker than mine.

"He's with me," I said before clarifying. "For now."

Badb rolled her eyes. "Then fuck him already so I can kill him and be done with it."

Gods. She and Nemain were so much alike.

"I need to speak with Nemain. Immediately." Technically, Pele should get the information first, since she was the one who asked me to gather it, but I needed to explain the Niall situation to Nemain.

I realized the significance of me prioritizing his safety over everything else, but I didn't feel like analyzing what that meant right now.

"She's busy." Badb leaned back against the wall and crossed her arms. "Tell me what you learned in the seraphim realm and what that fae asshole is doing with you."

My muscles protested and threatened to give out on me, but I hid the pain from my face as I rose from the bed and moved to stand in front of Badb. She was tall, but I had several inches on her and probably a good forty pounds of muscle.

I matched her position and crossed my arms while letting my wings spread out a little.

"I don't answer to you."

"You really want to push me, valkyrie?" She tilted her head in a purely feline gesture. "In my own damn house, no less?"

"About that…" I made a show of peering around the room and out the window that overlooked the main street of Emerald Bay. "Does Nemain know that you have a home here? In *her* town? Seems odd after her specifically telling you and Kalen that she wanted a bit of space."

Badb went absolutely still. Busted.

I let out a low laugh. "That's what I thought."

"We had no choice," she snarled. "Nemain is being foolish and stubborn by remaining here. She should move to the fae realms where we can better protect her."

I raised a brow. "You mean the way that Finn's village was protected?"

"That was different," Badb said through clenched teeth. "That attack came out of nowhere. Nemain could live at one of the Unseelie Queen's properties. There is no way Lir could reach her or Finn there."

"How do you still not know your daughter?" I shook my head. "Are you even making an effort to get to know her? Or are you too busy sneaking behind her back and defying her wishes?"

Her lips curled back over her teeth. "*Watch it.*"

"For all you know, there are Balor sympathizers in the fae

courts. Pele placed a ward around this entire town so that we know whenever a warlock, devourer, or vampire crosses the boundary. And the wards she's put in place around Nemain's apartment building are probably on par with the ones around your precious queen's home."

"I acknowledged that, which is why we are here," she ground out.

"But you didn't *tell* Nemain you were here." I leaned forward. "This is exactly why she's always pissed at you. You're always doing things behind her back. Even if you have her best intentions in mind, it still comes across as deceptive. It's a very fae thing to do."

"She's half fae," Badb pointed out stubbornly.

I sighed. Badb and Nemain were two sides of the same coin, and I had no idea how they were ever going to get along. Honestly, I didn't know how Kalen handled having a mate and a daughter this ridiculously stubborn.

"You won't tell her, will you?" For the first time ever, I saw uncertainty in Badb's eyes. "About us having an apartment here?"

"She is my friend. I will not lie to her about this."

Anger flashed across Badb's features, but also resignation. She knew this would be one more mark against her in Nemain's eyes.

A twinge of guilt hit me. I still felt that Badb and Kalen were going about this the wrong way, but I had no doubt that they loved their daughter. With a sigh, I added, "I'll give you the chance to tell her first. She should hear it from you. Besides, sooner or later she's gonna figure it out. This town isn't that big."

Badb snorted. "True enough."

"Now, will you please tell me where she is?" I stepped back, giving her more space. "I really do have important information to give her, and I need to do it soon so I can get this sorted out."

Green eyes latched onto the arm I'd carefully raised. The dark magic had receded, but I could already feel it seeping out again.

"I dragged a fae healer here for you." She gestured towards my arm. "They did the best they could, but they couldn't get rid of whatever the hell that dark magic is, only knock it back."

Fuck. There was still a chance that Kaysea could do it, but my confidence in that was pretty low. Any healer Badb summoned would have been someone she knew from the Unseelie Court, which meant they were likely powerful.

Alarm slammed into me when I realized that meant a sidhe had been here and I still hadn't seen Niall.

"Did they seem him?" I stepped quickly towards the door, yanking it open.

"See who?" Badb asked innocently as I stomped into the living room, blinking at the sunlight pouring in through the windows directly into my eyes.

I whirled around to face her. "Don't get cute with me, Morrigan."

"Oh? We're using official titles now, are we?" She smirked at me knowingly. "Do you prefer me to call you by your title? I did some digging into you while you were gone. Does one bow to valkyrie royalty?" She tapped a clawed fingertip against her lips. "Bowing doesn't seem like a valkyrie thing. Maybe thump my hand against my chest a few times?"

I was one second away from throttling her when the door swung open and Kalen walked in, followed by Niall. Relief at seeing him whole and unharmed rushed through me, but I was careful to keep it off my face.

I wasn't entirely sure what I was going to do about my growing attachment to Niall. I had no idea if he felt the same.

He flirted with me, and I'd definitely seen desire in his eyes, but that didn't mean he was feeling this all-consuming need like I was. For all I knew, he was going to settle things with Nemain and then leave, maybe help her from afar.

The thought of him leaving felt like a cold hand wrapping around my heart and squeezing.

"You're alright." Relief flooded Niall's face, and he cleared the distance between us in an instant. He took my arm into his hands, a deep crease forming between his brows. He twisted to face Badb but didn't release the gentle hold he had on me. "You said the fae healer could fix it. I agreed to leave, you agreed to heal her."

"You calling me a liar?" A dangerous glint lit up Badb's eyes. "Considering I promised to kill you if I ever saw you again, I suppose it would be to your benefit if I was one."

Kalen smoothly slid in-between his mate and Niall, his calm and patient mask firmly in place. But I'd seen him cut loose in the seraphim realm. I knew the monster that lurked underneath that mask.

"I'm sure the fae healer did the best they could," Niall said evenly. "But seidr magic doesn't play nicely with fae magic. Sigrun will need to find a healer in the Yggradsil realms to fully heal. But we've bought her some time."

"Spoilsport," Badb murmured as Kalen swung an arm across her shoulders and pulled her close.

Badb leaned into his touch and inhaled his scent like he was a delicious piece of steak she was thinking about inhaling. An odd pang hit me. In my over two thousand years of existence, I was beginning to realize that I'd never been in love.

Not like Kalen and Badb clearly were. Or like Mikhail and Nemain. Not that those two would ever admit it. Even Bryn, who had barely been alive for two decades, was madly in love with Elisa.

It was easy to ignore what you were missing when it wasn't in front of you constantly.

Whatever. I was fine. I just needed to get my arm healed, get my head on straight, and then find Gullveig and kill the shit out of her. I'd feel better and more like myself then.

"If I may…" I straightened and pulled my arm from Niall's grasp. "I would impose on you for two more things."

Badb rolled her eyes at my formality, but Kalen smiled. "Anything for a friend of our daughter."

"I'm not able to open a gateway to the Yggdrasil realms. If you could open one to Asgard, preferably close to the valkyrie stronghold, I would be in your debt."

"Yes. Fine." Badb waved off my request. She grumbled something else under her breath, but I couldn't quite hear it.

"Thank you." I kept my gaze locked on hers as I made my next request. "Would you mind keeping Gunnar and Viggo in your company while I attend to things in Asgard?"

WHAT?! Viggo protested loudly in my mind at the same time Gunnar's deep growl rumbled through the room.

"I'm sorry, my friends." I looked both Viggo and Gunnar in the eye. "It's time for me to meet with the Valkyrie Queen. I've put it off for as long as possible, but I can't any longer. There are many in the valkyrie stronghold who wish me ill, you would both be targeted if you came with me."

And I would kill any who raised a hand against you. I left those words unsaid, knowing that they would understand.

"They are more than welcome to stay with us," Kalen replied with a polite smile.

"I'm coming with you," Niall said firmly.

"Absolutely not."

"I'm not asking for permission," he said stubbornly. "You need someone to watch your back. I'm coming with you."

I looked to Kalen and Badb for support, but they were watching us with wide eyes like this was the best entertainment they'd seen in a while.

"Do I really need to remind you that you're a fae tainted with devourer magic?" I growled.

He shrugged. "You'll protect me."

I clenched my teeth together as I tilted my head back and stared at the ceiling. Murder. That was the only solution. I needed to kill him, and it would solve a good amount of my problems.

"Given that you are an exile," Kalen said, "it would be foolish of you to go alone. And the Yggdrasil realms have never been attacked by devourers, so they don't have the same baggage as the rest of the realms. I myself have traveled there several times, and I never had any issues."

"You are the Erlking." I pinched the bridge of my nose. "Nobody in their right mind is going to fuck with the Wild Hunt. And definitely not after you made that bitch your mate."

"Wow," Badb mused. "From 'The Morrigan' to 'that bitch' in less than ten minutes. I feel *so* honored."

I suddenly had a lot of understanding for why Nemain was so pissed off at her parents all the time. They were gods-damned exhausting.

Kalen raised a black sphere the size of his fist in the air. "You can record a message for Nemain and leave your findings with us. I promise you I will get it to her and guard over your friends while Badb escorts you and Niall to Asgard."

Badb looked at me with a smirk while Niall crossed his arms and glared at me stubbornly. I sighed and swiped the memory sphere from Kalen.

"Fine." I walked over to the small sitting area they set up in the cozy living room and plunked the chunk of glass down onto the table. "We'll leave in fifteen minutes."

This was going to be a disaster.

Chapter Nine

"We're here," I said flatly. "You can leave now."

My mood had only continued to sour after Niall declared he was coming with me.

After recording everything I had learned in the memory sphere and handing over the map and other notes to Kalen, we'd argued for ten minutes about all the reasons he should remain in Emerald Bay.

He wanted me to vouch for him to Nemain, and I did that in the recording.

When I pointed that out and the fact that Kalen could take him to Nemain, he'd just given me an amused smile.

"There is a very real chance that if I walk into a forest with Kalen, I won't walk out of it."

I'd frowned and looked at Kalen. They'd already been alone together, and Kalen hadn't attacked him. Badb was the one who still seemed keen on killing him.

"He speaks the truth," Kalen said, those obsidian black eyes focusing on the fae warrior, and Niall shifted beneath the weight of his gaze. "My mate wants you dead. And I'm inclined to agree with her. My soft-hearted daughter might forgive you, so perhaps it is for the best we never give her the chance."

I'd scoffed at him referring to Nemain as "soft-hearted". I'd seen the shifter brutally kill beings as they begged for their lives, and she'd done so with no hesitation and slept like a baby afterward.

My instincts told me that while there was some truth to Kalen's words, he was also playing a different angle.

For some reason, he wanted Niall to go with me, and this was his way of manipulating me into doing it.

Fucking fae.

Now, I just had to deal with Kalen's other half.

Who was slightly less manipulative but infinitely more insane. Great.

Badb smirked at me. She wore her long, feathered black cloak and had at least half a dozen blades strapped to her body that I could see. Probably many more hidden.

The Morrigan in all her glory.

"Oh? And what exactly is your plan here? Just going to stroll on in?" She raised a hand towards the imposing fortress that sat in front of the large mountain range before us.

The fortress, Heiðra Eilífa, served as the main stronghold of the valkyrie, and its walls had never been breached. Not even during Ragnarok. A bustling village surrounded the stone walls, and we were standing on the cusp of it, already attracting stares from the locals.

Most of them were Aesir, with a few elves and dwarves mixed in. The Aesir were similar in appearance to humans, they were just *more*. They had taller and stronger builds. Their hair had a luster to it that practically glowed in sunlight. And their skin that came in a variety of tones always had a richness to it.

Most of the Aesir were on par with humans when it came to innate magic abilities. The difference was that Aesir practiced and used their magic on a regular basis whereas most humans had no idea it existed.

The valkyries had a strong connection to the Aesir, as they were the ones we had bonded with the most over the course of our existence. I myself had bonded with one. The Valkyrie Queen shared a bond with one as well.

I hoped he wasn't in residence because the last time we'd seen each other, he'd been the one leading the party to tear me apart.

The queen hadn't stopped him.

Apprehension filled me as I stared up at the fortress. The valkyries guarding the walls already knew I was here; I could practically feel their hostility from where I stood. The flurry of activity around the village died down as the residents retreated to their homes, as they sensed the growing tension in the air.

I hadn't made it through the gates in my last attempt to meet with the queen, although I'd felt her watching me from the top of her tall tower where her throne was located.

I couldn't help but wonder if she was watching me now. If she had already given the order to kill me, burn my body, and scatter the ashes. Maybe she figured she'd eventually find a way to wipe me from existence and remove the stain of me from her legacy.

A deep pain throbbed in my chest, and only some of it was from the dark magic that was once again creeping in from the nidling bite. My feet remained firmly rooted in place, and I couldn't convince myself to take a step, even though I knew I had to. It was a mistake to come here.

"Calm yourself," Badb instructed. "As it happens, I do actually have a reason for being here. The Valkyrie Queen has refused to respond to the numerous messages my queen has sent her. I'm overdue for paying her a little visit."

"You could have mentioned that before," I growled.

Badb shrugged. "I'm mentioning it now."

"Perhaps we can table this conversation for now?" Niall said, his eyes glued to the top of the fortress walls. "We're about to have company."

Two valkyries leapt into the air and flew down to us. I didn't recognize them, but that wasn't surprising since there were a lot of new generations of valkyries that I'd never met. They both bore the same sharp cheekbones and thin lips. Definitely twins, which was fairly common amongst our kind. Their black hair was braided back, making their sharp features stand out even more. Identical light brown eyes looked at me with scorn.

Niall took a step forward; he didn't draw any weapons, but he positioned himself slightly between me and them. I didn't know if I appreciated the gesture as a sign of support and protection or if I was pissed off for him putting himself in harm's way.

I was beginning to understand Nemain's often irrational reactions to Mikhail.

"Hiding behind a fae?" the one on the left spat, disgust rolling off them both in palpable waves. "It appears you've fallen even further, Sigrun."

"We should rip those wings from your back," the other twin growled. "You're not a valkyrie. You're filth that refuses to die."

Generations separated me from these valkyries. They hadn't been alive during Ragnarok, and they had no idea what had been sacrificed. But every new generation passed down their hatred of me. I was the abomination that they refused to forget.

This was what I wanted to protect Bryn from. Why I'd been so pissed off at Nemain for bringing her to me.

Because even after everything the valkyries had done to me after Ragnorok, they were still my people. I still remembered what it was like to belong to them. To be respected and loved.

Bryn could have had that. Instead, she had chosen me. A

part of me feared that one day she would regret her choice, and that I'd see the same hate and disgust in her eyes that I witnessed in these two young valkyries.

I opened my mouth to say that we should leave, but Badb strolled forward, an easy, predatory gait to her movements as she stopped in front of the guards.

"I have business with the queen," she said, her lips curling into a warning sneer. "Run along, *children*."

"Who the fuck do you think you are?" The twin who had first spoken snarled and drew her sword, holding it to Badb's throat. Her sister drew her weapon as well but kept it angled at Niall and me.

"Don't kill them," I said quickly. No matter how much they hated me, I could never bring myself to return it.

"You and Kalen are always ruining my fun," she sighed.

Confusion flashed across both twins' faces, but before they could do anything, Badb knocked the sword from her throat and whipped her elbow into the valkyrie's face.

Bone crunched and blood poured from the broken nose. In another move too fast to track, Badb gripped the valkyrie's arm and twisted it, tearing ligaments and pulling it out of its socket. The sword slipped from the guard's fingers and Badb snatched it up, slamming the hilt into the girl's head.

She collapsed to the ground in a soundless heap.

"Tora!" the remaining valkyrie screamed and lunged forward to get between her fallen sister and Badb.

"You're lucky I'm here on official business," Badb said lightly. "And that the only valkyrie in existence I respect told me not to kill you."

Surprise flickered through me at Badb's words. While Kalen was more than happy to twist words into pretty little lies, Badb always spoke the truth.

The dark-haired valkyrie swung her sword at Badb, and I couldn't help but mentally critique her attack.

Valkyries weren't trained to ignore our feelings; rather, the opposite. Anger and fear could be used to hone your instincts and give you an edge in battle. But we were trained how to use those feelings and not simply attack based on them.

Whoever had trained these two had done a sloppy job of it. Bryn had been training with me for less than a year, but she was already far more skilled than them.

Niall and I watched as Badb disarmed the remaining valkyrie within seconds and now held both swords against the girl's throat.

"I think," Badb said, an edge punctuating her voice, "I'm the *fucking* Morrigan. And you should probably know who you're facing before you mouth off."

She took a step back and flipped the swords around, handing them hilt-first back to the valkyrie.

The girl snatched them out of her hands, but I could see in her eyes that she was about to have another go against Badb.

"Not very bright, are you?" Niall tsked, drawing the valkyrie's ire.

"Alruna!" a deep voice snapped as another valkyrie landed in front of us.

This one I recognized immediately. Eylif. The Valkyrie Queen's second-in-command. She didn't look at me or Niall, but I could feel the disgust rolling off her.

"The queen will see you know." Eylif didn't give us a chance to respond before turning back around and stalking towards the gates that slowly opened for us.

Badb's bright green eyes fell on me, almost amused. "Valkyries. So welcoming."

As we walked through Heiðra Eilífa and I felt the cold glare of every valkyrie on me, I was glad I had forced Gunnar and

Viggo to remain behind. They were both pissed off at me. Viggo had refused to speak to me, and Gunnar had even growled at me when I tried to pet him before leaving.

But anyone who stood beside me was a target, and if I lost my stoic wolf or my brazen feline, I didn't know what I would do.

Actually, I knew exactly what I would do. I would kill whoever harmed them, even if they were valkyries. And I knew that would be the final wound that shattered my soul.

Badb strolled beside me as if she didn't have a care in the world. She grinned tauntingly at the valkyries who sneered at us as we passed and let out a low laugh whenever they mouthed off to her.

But underneath her amused exterior was a predator lurking. One that hoped a valkyrie would try and mess with her so that she could show them her fangs and claws.

The Morrigan was here. And she was always spoiling for a fight.

Whatever Niall was feeling, he hid it well, but I noticed the tightening at the corners of his mouth.

I snuck glances at him as we made our way through the wide cobblestone streets, and I felt him do the same. But whenever I looked at him, his eyes were ahead of us, assessing any potential threats.

The charming fae who had been my companion these last few days was nowhere to be seen.

"You alright?" I finally asked.

Three stone towers rose in front of us. The one in the center was the tallest, and even from here I could make out the large arched openings at the top that allowed valkyries to fly in. Bridgeways made of rich cedar wood and stone so dark it was almost black spanned the distance between the center tower and the two that flanked it. The entire structure looked wildly unstable, but it had originally been built by the dwarves and each of those stones dripped in magic.

Jörmungandr himself could crash into those towers and they would simply bounce the World Serpent away.

This was the heart of Heiðra Eilífa, where the Valkyrie Queen waited for us.

Finally, Niall turned to face me, and I halted when I saw the mixture of sorrow and devastation in his eyes.

"What's wrong?" Without realizing it, I took a step forward and instinctively raised my hand to his face.

Before I could pull it away, he laid his hand over mine and held it there. The warmth of his skin felt like a jolt to my system, and I could have sworn the dark magic fighting through my body shirked away from it.

"They hate you," he said slowly. Those sharp blue eyes that seemed to miss nothing flicked over the valkyries around us before focusing back on me. "They're your people. And they *hate* you."

"Not my people," I said sadly, feeling as though a knife twisted in my heart. "I don't belong anywhere anymore."

Niall's troubled expression only grew more so. I'd given him the brief overview of my history with the valkyries, but clearly, he hadn't been expecting this level of vitriol.

"Valkyrie!" Badb barked from where she waited further up the street with our escort. "Don't waste your time on those who aren't worthy. You belong with us. Personally, I think you traded up."

Damn shifter hearing.

The valkyries who had been passing us by stopped, and the already tense mood intensified. I saw more than a few hands inch closer to their weapons, and Badb only grinned wider.

Up until this moment, I thought Nemain took the prize for being the most insane. But Badb seemed more than happy to throw down with the valkyries in their own damn stronghold.

Clearly, my previous assessment had been wrong.

Despite how much it pissed me off that the valkyries were judging me for having to make an impossible choice, one that they ultimately benefited from, I didn't want to see any of them dead.

"Come on." I slipped my hand free from Niall's and grabbed his arm, tugging him forward. "Let's not keep the queen waiting."

The hostility aimed our way didn't wain, but no one made a move towards us either, so I considered that a win.

We walked the remaining distance in silence as I took in the place that had once been my home. While the village outside these walls had expanded greatly, the main part of Heiðra Eilífa remained the same as I remembered it.

The three towers looming ahead of us were where the queen and the higher ranking valkyries lived. The rest lived in the simple but comfortable cottages made of wood and stone. Most had flower baskets hanging beneath their windows adding splashes of color. There were a few trees here and there, but they were carefully spaced so that they wouldn't interfere with valkyries flying in or out.

It hadn't been my intention, but the cottage I'd built in the realm I'd been living in the last few centuries was almost identical to the ones here.

I was a terrible gardener, so I didn't have any window planters, but I'd specifically chosen the location because of the wildflowers that grew in the surrounding meadow. The faint sound of metal clanging against metal came from behind the towers where the training grounds were.

Before Ragnarok, that was where I had spent most of my time, training the future generation. It was what I missed the most from my old life. But having Bryn eased that pain now.

Soon, we stood before doors made of solid gold that

towered above us. Carved into them was Yggdrasil, the tree of life, its branches reaching out to all nine realms.

Badb's lip curled. "I thought the fae were impractical. Gold? Really?"

"Badb," I said, my voice strained.

She rolled her eyes but kept the rest of her comments to herself. Niall's lips twitched, amusement lighting up his eyes.

"Don't start," I warned.

"I would never." He gave me a hurt expression, and I let out a long-suffering sigh.

Eylif barked a command, and the doors swung open.

"The queen is waiting for you." Eylif gave me a cold smile. "In the lower throne room."

My body stiffened before I could stop it, and Eylif's smile grew wider, happy she hit her mark. Niall gave me a questioning look, but I only shook my head, not wanting to explain the intricacies of valkyrie culture to him. Not here.

Later, I'd tell him that the lower throne room was where the queen greeted outsiders only.

While Badb and him might qualify as such, technically if they were traveling with the company of a valkyrie, they should be elevated to the upper throne room at the top of the tower.

This was the queen's not so subtle way of reminding me of my place. I should be used to it by now. But it was one thing to be hated by the valkyries in general.

Quite another thing to be hated by your own *mother*.

Chapter Ten

IT'S odd the way memory works. The familiar sights as we'd walked through Heiðra Eilífa had tugged at my mind, but I'd let the thoughts drift in and out like the tide.

But as soon as we passed through those gilded doors, the familiar scent of juniper and wild herbs almost brought me to my knees. The earthy incense burned throughout this tower and clung to your skin and clothes long after you left.

It was the smell of home.

A part of me broke at the realization, and I stumbled as the dark magic seized the opportunity to regain the ground it had lost earlier at Niall's touch. Only the fae warrior's grip on my arm kept me from falling.

"You've grown weak, daughter," a strong voice announced.

"Daughter?" Niall looked at the tall valkyrie who waited for us in front of another set of ornate doors, these already pulled open to display the throne room beyond.

Ignoring the sharp pain in my chest, I straightened to my full height and held my head high. "Hello, Mother."

"I didn't think it was possible for you to disgrace yourself more. But here you stand"—she made a point of looking both

Niall and Badb up and down, distaste causing her features to pinch together—"clutching the arm of a devourer freak while the shifter whore stands at your side. Such a disappointment you turned out to be."

The Valkyrie Queen turned and headed into the throne room as if she couldn't stand to look at me a second longer.

I had been prepared for my mother's vitriol but even then, the look of absolute revulsion in her eyes hurt far more than the hateful words she had spewed.

A breath rattled in my chest as my lungs struggled against the dark magic that was doing its best to choke them. It looked like my short reprieve thanks to the healing session from the fae was coming to an end.

If my mother denied me help, I'd have to hope that Kaysea was strong enough to heal me or at least buy me more time. Maybe the daemons could assist me. Healing magic wasn't their forte, but they knew their way around dark magic. Whoever I went to, my time was running out. This needed to be mended, and fast.

"What the fuck was that?" Niall growled, his eyes locked on the open doors that my mother had passed through.

"My mother," I said lightly. "She's a real charmer."

"Your mum's a bitch." Badb chuckled; something about the sound was distinctly feline. "I will say it gives me hope for my relationship with Nemain. Suddenly, our relationship looks downright healthy."

"She tried to gut you last time you were in the room together," I said dryly.

"Yeah." Badb gave me a quick grin. "But the threat of violence is a statement of love in our family."

I snorted. "This is why Elisa says we all need therapy."

"She's just saying that because she's become friends with that empath girl." Badb waved me off.

We were still standing in the entrance hallway, and I appreciated that they were giving me time to brace myself before entering the throne room.

And doing round two with my mother.

"What's therapy?" Niall's attention fell back on me, his eyebrows bunched together.

"According to Nemain, it's whiskey," I said, finally cracking a smile. "Let's get this over with."

Niall and I fell in line beside Badb. She was the one here on official business, after all. Once she was done, I'd speak my piece about Gullveig and also ask for help with the nidling bite.

Given the warm reception I'd received thus far, I wasn't holding my breath to get any help, but there was still a chance. While my mother might hate me, as the Valkyrie Queen she couldn't be ruled by her emotions. I'd just need to convince her that it was worth healing me so that I would be in fighting shape against Gullveig.

No guards were posted outside the throne room. Nobody made it this far unless the queen wanted to see them, and she was more than capable of protecting herself.

Badb lazily waltzed through the room to where my mother waited for us on her elaborate gold throne. I couldn't see Badb's face, but I imagined she was wearing a sneer at the ridiculous show of opulence.

But gold was common here and across most of the Yggdrasil realms. On its own, it was too soft to use for weapons, but like silver, gold readily absorbed magic. Most of the weapons crafted in Yggdrasil had gold plating or engravings that strengthened them with magic. The fae did the same, but they preferred to use silver.

This throne had been made by the dwarves thousands of years ago. Two crossed axes rose from the back of the chair above my mother's head, a nod to her preferred weapon in battle.

This throne had been made for her, and she had fought off all challengers for almost three thousand years.

I wasn't sure how much Badb knew about my mother. If she even knew the valkyrie who looked no older than nineteen was close to the fae queens in age. The way Niall's gaze kept bouncing between me and the Valkyrie Queen, I knew he was trying to see bits of my mother in me and failing.

The only thing we had in common was our rich dark brown skin. My mother was several inches shorter than me with a leaner build. The brown eyes that looked at me with such disdain were several shades lighter than mine, and they sat on a pretty face with delicate features.

The Valkyrie Queen was stunning. It was easy to forget that she was a warrior who had survived multiple wars.

I was beautiful, but no one would ever mistake me as anything other than a warrior. That was the first thing they saw. And often the last.

Despite her age, my mother carried a youthfulness about her. She had risen as a valkyrie on her nineteenth birthday, whereas I was almost thirty before I had chosen to rise. It had been one of the many choices that had annoyed my mother. A valkyrie didn't come fully into her powers until she died a mortal death and woke to an immortal life. But I hadn't been in a hurry, and at nineteen I had been tall and gangly.

By my early twenties, I had filled out, but then stubborn-ness had set in, and I had wanted to defy my mother.

Even before Ragnarok sent me on a path there was no coming back from, our mother-daughter relationship had been strained. It was hard being the daughter of the first and only Valkyrie Queen.

It was even harder being the *exiled* daughter of one.

"Greetings, Róta." Badb swaggered up to the throne, stopping a few feet away. "Thanks for the warm welcome. I can just *feel* the generous hospitality in my soul."

"It's Queen Róta to you," Eylif snapped from where she'd taken up a position behind the throne.

My mother held up a hand to silence her second-in-command, but I could tell Badb's fragrant disrespect irked her. It was probably petty of me, but I took a little joy in that.

"*Queen* Elvina"—my mother's eyes narrowed further at the emphasized use of *queen*—"wishes to know why you haven't responded to her request." Badb had the audacity to inspect her nails as she if was already bored with this conversation.

"Because my answer hasn't changed since the last time she offered," Róta said tightly. "We're not afraid of the devourers, nor do we fear this exiled fae king that has them so concerned. If they come to these realms, we'll slaughter them all."

"Not all devourers are so easily dispatched." Badb's eyes flicked up from her nails to peer at the Valkyrie Queen. "Your people will die by the thousands."

"Then the halls of Valhalla will rejoice in welcoming their fallen brethren." I sucked in a sharp inhale as my mother leaned back in her throne, as if she was completely unbothered by this possibility.

"And what of the regular people?" I demanded, the rage in me causing the breath in my lungs to rattle against the dark magic squeezing them. "Will Valhalla welcome the farmers who die in such slaughter? The artisans? The elves who have sworn off violence?"

"There are always causalities in war." Róta's sharp gaze cut to me.

"You may be known as the Valkyrie Queen," Badb said coldly, "but it was my understanding that after Ragnarok, you came to be the queen of *all* the Yggdrasil realms. Is that not true?"

The Aesir had never fully recovered from losing the most powerful among them. Sooner or later, I was sure some would rise to challenge my mother. Even in my exile, I'd heard whispers of those who were unhappy with the rule of the Valkyrie Queen.

My mother sat on her throne with a bored expression, completely unmoved by our words. I shouldn't have expected any better.

Frustration and anger made my blood boil. Even though Yggdrasil was no longer my home, and the valkyries would kill me if they could, I'd never turn my back on these realms. I may be an exile, but I still cared about the people of Yggdrasil. Apparently, more so than their queen.

"What is it that the fae queens are offering?" I twisted to face Badb, who was staring at my mother like she was contemplating slitting her throat.

"Placing a protective ward around Vanaheim and Asgard in exchange for an alliance against Balor," Badb said. "Standard stuff, promises to fight against him, not offering safe harbor to any of his ilk, trade deals that benefit both sides. The documents detailing everything were sent here months ago."

"All the realms," I said firmly. "The fae queens will extend the protective ward around *all* the Yggdrasil realms."

Something flickered in Badb's eyes, and she hesitated. "That means they'd have to ward eight realms instead of two. That would require a lot more power."

"Vanaheim and Asgard are the realms most likely to survive against an army of devourers. The other realms are primarily made up of peaceful people who will not stand a chance. It's all the realms or none of them."

Badb pursed her lips but jerked her head in a nod. "Deal."

"Deal?" Róta laughed coldly. "There is no deal. *I am queen.* My daughter has never spoken for me before, and she certainly does not now."

"You will do this," I said in a tone that left no room for argument. The air around us grew charged with static, and Eylif shifted uneasily.

"I will not." My mother rose from her throne and closed the distance between us. "Neither you nor that blasphemous weapon you carry frightens me. You are barely standing. A few more minutes and the only thing you'll be capable of doing is lying on the ground, whimpering from pain as the dark magic ravages your body."

She wasn't wrong. Only my rage was keeping me upright at this point. Every single tendon felt like it was being shredded, and every breath felt like fire in my lungs.

"Gullveig is back." I raised my chin and fought against the trembling that was starting to stir in my muscles.

My mother's eyes narrowed. "This is your desperate attempt to get me to agree? A pathetic lie?" she scoffed.

"Not lying," I ground out. "I've spoken to her. She possessed a Vanir girl and came to my realm." I left out her recent possession of the seraph because Niall didn't know about that, and I had no doubt he would react poorly to the news. "All these centuries, she's been collecting followers and plotting."

"I destroyed her once, and I can do so again."

"At what cost?" I sucked in a painful breath.

Niall was suddenly at my back, wordlessly giving me support.

I let myself lean against him, trusting him to not let me fall. "Last time, she recruited valkyries to her side. She's likely to do so again. Are you prepared to kill valkyries again, Mother?"

My words struck true, and she inhaled a sharp breath. For all my mother's faults, she loved her people—the valkyries. The civil war during Ragnarok had come close to breaking her. Her compassion towards the rest of the beings that called Yggdrasil home was far more tenuous.

"What are you proposing?" she asked tightly.

"Heal me." Darkness encroached on my vision, and I

leaned more of my weight against Niall, one of his arms snaking around my waist. "I will kill her once and for all."

"And if you fall?" There was no hint of sorrow in her voice, merely a queen considering backup plans.

"Then I will," Badb said smoothly. "Agree to the deal, and we will see to it that Gullveig dies. And stays dead this time."

After a few beats of silence, the Valkyrie Queen looked at me. "Deal."

For the second time in less than twenty-four hours, I passed out.

Awareness slowly crept back in. My wings were wrapped around me like a cloak, and I was cocooned in soft fabric. An arm was draped across my chest, pulling me back against a warm body.

Grogginess still tugged at me, but I opened my eyes and blinked a few times to clear them.

A familiar room welcomed me, and I looked at it with an odd sort of detachment. The large bed took up most of the space, and the frame was made of the same dark, rich wood that the floor and walls were.

There wasn't much in the way of personal possessions in the room, aside from two paintings on the wall. One was of me in my early twenties with two other valkyries.

A tall blonde with ice-blue eyes, high cheekbones, and full lips that were always fixed in a mischievous grin.

On my other side was a valkyrie with light brown skin, unruly russet brown hair that she usually wrestled back into a bun, and forest-green eyes that had always viewed the world with such inquisitiveness.

Herja and Skuld. Two of my best friends.

Both had perished during Ragnarok.

I stared at the painting for a few minutes. My last memory of them was finding them on the battlefield, almost burned beyond recognition, their lives already snuffed out.

I didn't want to remember them like that. I wanted to remember them as the friends I'd grown up with. The ones who hadn't been the least bit intimated by befriending the daughter of the Valkyrie Queen. Who hadn't treated me as a political steppingstone and instead had dragged me on one misadventure after another.

The arm around me shifted, and I blinked several times to clear the tears that where threatening to fall. Twisting around, I looked into Niall's light blue eyes that always saw too much.

"Hi," I said awkwardly.

It'd been a long time since I'd woken up with a man in my bed. We hadn't done anything, but that somehow made this more intimate.

"Hi," Niall said, a faint flush darkening across his cheeks, drawing a smile out of me.

"Going to tell me why you're in my bed?" I arched an eyebrow at him, and the color staining his cheeks deepened.

"The healer your mother sent in was able to rid you of the dark magic from the nidling bite," he said. "But they didn't heal your body. I got the impression it wasn't because they couldn't do that, but because the queen had only ordered you to be healed of the dark magic and nothing more."

I snorted. "Honestly, I'm surprised they didn't stab me after healing me."

He grimaced. "My presence might have been the reason for the lack of stabbing."

"Ah," I said and chewed on my bottom lip. Niall hadn't released me, and I hadn't pulled away either.

"This was your room?" His eyes scanned the space before lingering on the painting of me, Herja, and Skuld before going to the second painting. I didn't miss the hitch in his breathing as he took it in. "Who?"

My attention finally went to the space on the wall I'd been avoiding looking at since I woke up.

This one was also of me, although I'd been older. The painting was of the day I performed the ritual to rise as a valkyrie. I stood in front of a cliff, the sun cresting in the sky behind me.

In front of me was an impossibly tall and broad-shouldered man. We were both in profile, but he still exuded strength.

Even in the painting, there was something about him that pulled at you. In real life, that pull had been so much more intense. I wasn't the only one who felt it; so many had followed him, trusting him absolutely with their lives.

Other memories may have faded, but I remembered that day perfectly. Standing there, in nothing but a thin shift with my braids loose around me. For once, he had let his own blond hair fall to his shoulders instead of tying it back. Deep blue eyes had looked at me with love and devotion as he held a dagger to my heart.

"I choose you, Sigrun. And I accept this bond."

"I choose you, Thor. And I accept this bond."

As if my body remembered that day, my hand moved to rest over my heart. It remembered Thor slipping that dagger into me. My life blood pouring out as he held me before I took a few wobbling steps to the cliff and let myself fall.

And rose as a valkyrie. Bonded to the most powerful Aesir to ever walk the realms.

"It's not what you think," I said softly. "His name was Thor Odinson, and he wasn't my lover. But he was the beginning and end of me in so many ways."

"I think I can understand that." Niall looked at me, meeting my eyes with his own, and I believed him.

Our situations might be different, but he understood what it was like to give yourself to someone completely and then have to piece yourself back together when that fell apart.

There were some wounds that you had to heal on your own. Pieces of your soul that only you could truly restore.

But what I'd failed to realize in my long life was that sometimes other people could help you with those broken pieces. My mother rejected me. The valkyries no longer wanted me.

But that didn't mean I was alone, nor did it mean I had to continue existing with a shattered existence.

I had the unyielding loyalty and love of so many. Gunnar and Viggo. Nemain and Magos. Mikhail would follow those two anywhere.

And Bryn. My stubborn but resilient apprentice who had known enough about me to know that choosing me meant never joining the valkyries. Meant never finding out who her mother had been.

She'd known all that… and still chosen me.

Niall had chosen me. I felt the truth of it in my soul. It didn't matter that we'd only known each other for barely a week.

The intensity of my feelings for him had once frightened me. But now that I accepted them, that fear slipped away, and instead I only felt how right this was.

He was the last piece I had been missing.

"Hjartað mitt. *My heart.*" I raised a hand to cup his face, and he leaned it without ever taking his eyes off me. "I'm ready for a new beginning if you are."

Niall went still beneath my touch, something dark and hollow flitting through his eyes before he blinked and it was gone. That glimpse of something wrong that I'd occasionally see before he'd hide it away from me.

I opened my mouth to question him, but the words died on

my lips as he ran his fingers across my jawline before cupping the back of my neck and pulling me close.

"Deal," he promised before his lips crashed against mine.

Chapter Eleven

THE AWKWARDNESS of waking up in the bed with Niall was gone, as was the sweetness from our conversation.

His mouth on mine was demanding. So were my hands pulling him closer to me.

I'd already been stripped down to my base layers, and thankfully Niall had done the same before crawling into bed with me. If I'd had to deal with laces and buckles right now, I probably would have screamed.

My hands slipped under his shirt, greedily exploring the ridges of muscles across his abs before dragging my fingers across his strong back. Niall leaned further over me, nipping my bottom lip before sucking it into his mouth. At the same moment, his hand squeezed my breast while roughly running his thumb over the nipple.

"Fucking hell," I moaned.

I wanted to feel his skin against mine. *Now.*

Niall clearly felt the same, as he tugged on the loose shift I was wearing while I ripped his shirt down the front and licked his chest.

"Fuck," he growled. "I didn't know that was an option."

In seconds, the thin fabric of the shift was torn away, and Niall grabbed one breast while sucking the other into his mouth. A sound somewhere between a moan and a whimper escaped from my lips as Niall clutched me harder against him while he licked, sucked, and stroked me.

I arched my back off the bed, giving him access and making it a little more comfortable for my wings.

Niall raised his head and eyed my wings, then in a smooth motion flipped us around so that I was straddling his thighs.

My wings stretched out over us, the bright sunlight hitting them and setting the golden feathers aglow.

"So fucking beautiful." Niall stared at them in wonder.

"You can look at them later." I gripped his chin, firmly drawing his attention back to my eyes. "You've got work to do, hjartað mitt."

"I'm at your mercy, álainn." The smile on his face was pure sin as he grabbed my waist and lifted me up until I was directly over his face.

Shock rippled through me at how easily he was able to pick me up, but that feeling along with every thought in my head emptied the moment his tongue licked a demanding stroke up my pussy before twirling around my clit.

My hands gripped the headboard, and I let my head fall back as quick pants slipped between my parted lips. My wings flaring even wider to help me balance.

Niall's hands gripped my ass as he continued to hold me over him and devour me.

If I had been capable of thinking, I probably would have been embarrassed by the mewling sounds he pulled out of me with every stroke of his tongue. My thighs started to tremble, and his fingers dug in even harder as his tongue dove in deep.

"*Niall.*" His name was but a mere whisper on my lips.

His mouth closed around my clit, and he sucked hard. My

climax crashed into me, and the headboard splintered beneath my grip.

Instead of letting up, Niall only continued feasting on me, further drawing out my euphoria.

Finally, my trembles started to fade, but before I could fully recover, the hands supporting me disappeared and my wings had to flap to keep me upright as my hands continued to clutch the headboard. I heard the sound of more fabric ripping, then those strong hands gripped my waist once more and moved me down until I was straddling his hips.

I barely had time to find my balance before Niall thrusted into me. A deep moan spilled past my lips at the sensation of feeling so perfectly full.

"You feel so goddamn amazing," he growled.

His eyes looked down at where we were joined together and darkened. The look of hunger on his face no doubt matched my own.

I spread my legs a little wider, and a groan of bliss came from us both as he sank even deeper inside.

"Fuck," I swore when he raised his hips. "We should have done this sooner."

"Yeah, we really should have," he agreed and wrapped a hand behind my neck, pulling me down to claim my mouth with his.

I could taste the echoes of my pleasure on his tongue when it slipped between my lips, and I greedily kissed him back. He trailed kisses along my jawline until he reached my throat, and I tilted my head to give him better access.

He groaned, "I wanted you the moment you held that knife to my throat." Hot breath tickled my skin, and my thighs clenched tighter.

I leaned back and planted my hands on his chest. Heat and need spiraled in my core as I rode him. His dark hair was spread out around him, making his brilliant blue eyes stand out even more.

Gods, he was gorgeous. And he was fucking *mine*.

"Show me how much you want me." I rocked my hips forward, eliciting a groan from him as his large hands gripped my waist. Every time I sped up, muscles along his jawline would flex, and he'd clamp onto me harder to slow down the pace.

"You're still healing," he said in a strained voice as he stubbornly kept himself in check.

"I'm fine." I let out a frustrated huff. "Fuck. Me."

My hands found the headboard once more, and I used the leverage to lift myself up, sliding his hard length almost all the way out and holding above him. Niall's fingers dug into my flesh as his eyes squeezed shut and a deep groan tumbled out of him.

A wicked grin stretched across my lips as I slowly, so fucking slowly, lowered myself back onto his cock.

"Gods…damn it," he ground out.

I let out a husky laugh and did it again. And again.

It was almost as torturous for me as it was for him, and I wanted nothing more than to slam back down and ride him hard. But I also desperately wanted to know what it was like for Niall to take control, so I kept up the teasing even as my body was aching for more.

"*Sigrun*," he warned.

"Yes?" I let out a breathy moan as I lowered myself once more and ground against him.

His eyes snapped open and in a flash, he ripped me off him. I hissed at the loss of feeling him inside me.

Before I could voice my complaints, he had me on all fours and slammed back into me. One hand dug into my hip while the other wrapped around my hair and yanked my head back.

The orgasm that had been just waiting on the edges

erupted, and I felt its aftermath drip down my inner thighs. Niall didn't stop.

He fucked me through it even as I screamed and trembled beneath him. Each stroke felt like it was deeper and faster than the one before it. My wings flared out to the sides, and even with his harsh thrusting, Niall easily maneuvered around them.

"You are fucking magnificent." Niall released the punishing grip on my hair so that he could grip my hips with both hands. "Do you like me being buried inside you?"

"Yes!" I screamed. My back arched as he hit a particularly sensitive spot, and my thoughts scattered.

"Good," he growled before wrapping an arm around my stomach and pulling me against his chest.

My wings flattened between us, and I realized at some point that he'd called his wings forth too because I could see black feathers out of the corners of my eyes. Fingers slid across my jaw, twisting my face around, and Niall's mouth crashed against mine.

It wasn't a kiss. It was a claiming. A promise.

He pulled back enough so that he could look into my eyes as if searching for an answer.

I let everything I was feeling show through them. My desire of him, body and soul. My fear of how much he meant to me. My love. Because that's what this was, and I wouldn't deny it. He saw it all, and when he kissed me softly, I knew he understood.

"Glad we're on the same page." He kissed the corners of my mouth. "Now, grab the fucking headboard."

I had to stretch forward to wrap my hands around the heavy wooden frame again.

Every muscle of my body was keyed up with tension, and trembles ran through me at the desperation to feel him moving inside me again.

He didn't keep me waiting long.

A cry tore out of my throat, and my body slid forward on the mattress as Niall thrusted back into me. Shudders racked my body as he pulled all the way out before doing it again. And again. He was punishing me for teasing him earlier.

I wanted to scream at him, but every time he slammed himself into me, my thoughts scattered, and only a breathy moan came out instead.

His large body leaned over mine, black wings folding over my golden ones, and I groaned as his teeth scraped my neck.

Slowly he eased his thick cock back in, and my nails dug into the headboard. Niall's hands wrapped around mine, and his hips rocked forward as he thrusted even deeper inside me.

"Niall," I half-moaned, half-screamed, unable to take any more of this.

His name on my lips was his undoing, and his hands gripped mine tighter as he pumped himself inside me, brutal and fast. I came so hard, my vision seemed to dim as Niall continued to piston his hips, slamming into me over and over again.

Even as the trembles of my orgasm faded, I felt the beginnings of another sliding into its place. Gods, I'd never come so many times in my life.

"Fuck," Niall hissed, his pace gaining a new savage edge.

The orgasm that had been building detonated, sending pleasure racing through my body seconds before Niall roared and emptied himself inside me.

We both sagged, still gripping the headboard with our wings draping down on either side of the bed. I felt the rapid beat of his heart against my back, and I decided there was no feeling I liked better.

"TELL ME ABOUT HIM," Niall murmured, his hand resting on my hip, drawing slow strokes with his fingers.

I was taking up most of the bed with my wings spread out beneath me while he was balanced on his side, propped up on an elbow. One of his wings was dangling off the bed while the other was extended over the two of us, lying across my legs.

I loved the feeling of his feathers against me, something he figured out very quickly and used to his advantage several times.

"Tell me about Balor," I countered. I knew the "him" Niall was referring to, and I wasn't sure if I was ready to talk about it. If I'd ever be ready to talk about it.

"A story for a story," Niall offered with a sly grin.

"Everything is a bargain with you fae," I grumbled.

Niall said nothing as he tenderly kissed my neck before leaning back with an expectant look on his face.

He wouldn't push. If I said I didn't want to talk about it, I knew he'd drop it. But he deserved to know, and I found myself not wanting to hide anything from him, despite how painful it would be to explain.

"Fine," I agreed and quickly held up a finger. His eyes lit up in excitement. "But this is going to be the short version."

"I find that quite acceptable," he said solemnly.

I rolled my eyes as I mentally attempted to piece together a shortened version of the events.

"In order for a valkyrie to come into the full range of our power, we have to bond with another individual. It's hard to explain how we know who to bond with." I paused, bunching my eyebrows together as I tried to think of what to say before shaking my head. "We just know."

Niall nodded in understanding. "The sciatháin get similar feelings when we find our mate."

My heartbeat quickened at the word *mate*, but I'd agreed to tell him my story and couldn't veer off course now.

"The Asgardians and Vanir have always had a bit of a history, mostly because Odin led the Asgardians, and he was an asshole. But the valkyries bonded with both and were a neutral party between the two realms. Thor was the son of Odin, and since I was the daughter of the Valkyrie Queen, the two of us crossed paths at an early age."

I smiled at the memory of a young boy with a mop of blond hair, racing down a hallway and slamming into me.

"He was a bit of a prankster when he was a kid and was always getting into trouble. Which meant *I* was always getting into trouble. My mother found it very unbecoming of a young valkyrie, but there wasn't anything she could do about it. It was clear to everyone that Thor and I would bond one day."

"It's hard to imagine a younger you getting into trouble." Niall chucked, shaking his head. "You're so *serious*."

"Like I said,"—a sad smile tugged at my lips—"Thor was the one getting into trouble. I was trying to keep him out of it but still got blamed."

Sensing the shift in my mood, Niall dropped a hand to my stomach and started tracing slow, lazy patterns.

I focused on the sensation and continued even though I hated what came next. "By the time we bonded, things were starting to heat up between the realms. Because of a prophecy."

"Nothing good ever comes from prophecy," Niall noted.

"It really doesn't," I agreed. "All of the seers throughout the Yggdrasil realms started having the same vision of the end of our realms—of Ragnarok. They saw the deaths of Odin, Thor, and many others. Everyone was worried about the prophecy, but Odin became obsessed with it, particularly about his own death. He started going after anyone who could potentially be a threat to him, and eventually civil war broke out. Mostly between the Asgardians and Vanir, but everyone was forced to choose a side."

"The valkyries couldn't remain neutral if they were bonded," Niall guessed. "Whatever side your bonded was on, you had to be on as well."

"Yes," I said, swallowing hard. "There were some bonded pairs who agreed to be neutral, but they were few and far between. Entire populations were being slaughtered by one side or the other, so many became involved simply to try and stop the carnage.

"Thor idolized his father. Many people did. Odin was skilled at speaking in a way that appealed directly to you. Like he could see into your mind and understand what you needed to hear to steer you onto the path he wanted. I tried to tell Thor that his father was manipulating him, but he refused to believe me."

An old pang tore through my heart. We'd had that fight many times over. Me trying to get Thor to see reason and him refusing to hear anything bad spoken about his father.

I'd been so angry. And he'd been so blind.

"My relationship with my mother was always strained, and he thought I was just acting out because of that." I closed my eyes and refocused on the soothing patterns Niall was still tracing on my skin. "Every day, I saw more and more of the man I knew slipping away and becoming something else."

The scene of a burned-down village flashed in my mind's eye. So vivid I could almost smell the charred flesh.

Niall raised the wing that had been lying across our legs over my chest like he could shield me from the pain. My fingers ran down the soft feathers, each one such a glorious inky black.

I inhaled his earthy scent and let myself bask in his warmth and comfort for a few minutes before continuing.

"The only people Odin hated more than the Vanir were the Jötnar, the giants of Jotunheim," I explained. "He convinced Thor that the Jötnar were the greatest threat to them, and that if they were wiped out, Ragnarok wouldn't happen and the realms would be saved."

"Sacrifice some to save many," Niall said. "Balor would often make similar claims."

"It was bullshit," I half snarled. "The Jötnar were mostly pacifists. Only a few of them had joined the fight against Odin, and that was because he drove them to it."

"And then he used their actions to justify further actions against all of the Jötnar?" he guessed.

"Yes," I said grimly. "By this point, Thor and I were arguing constantly. I was doing my best to stay out of the direct fighting, but I was still protecting him… which meant killing valkyries who went after him.

"I was close to my breaking point, and he knew it, so he waited until I was out on a mission and went to Jotunheim."

The words stuck in my throat. Even centuries later, the horror of what Thor had done still seemed impossible. It was hard to accept that the honorable and kind man I had known growing up was capable of such wholesale slaughter.

I raised my hand from Niall's chest, and the hammer obediently flew to it.

"Its name is Mjölnir," I said softly. "It was Thor's birthright, and only he could wield it because it contains the smallest fragment of his soul. He flew from city to city across Jotunheim and brought down storms upon all the Jötnar. In just a few days, he managed to wipe out almost the entire population."

I dropped Mjölnir to the floor, and it landed with a resounding thud.

Niall's brow furrowed. "Almost? Some survived?"

"The loki hid them," I nearly whispered the words. "The world thinks the Jötnar are dead, and most are, but the loki managed to save some of them."

"Why haven't they come out of hiding?" Niall frowned. "With Ragnarok over, isn't it safe for them?"

"I don't know." I shook my head. "It's a closely guarded secret."

"How do you know then?" He raised an eyebrow. "Given your status with Thor, I wouldn't think you would be on the top of their list for people to trust with this knowledge."

"Nemain," I said ruefully. "It's related to how we met actually. We had both picked up the same gig, and it inadvertently led us to where some of the loki were hiding a family of Jötnar. Nemain bargained on my behalf, and the loki agreed to let me go unharmed."

"That shifter leads an interesting life," Niall said.

I snorted. "She sticks her nose where she shouldn't and often fights when she should run."

"It's her feline nature." He shrugged.

"True." I gave a rueful shake of my head.

Niall went back to tracing patterns against my skin before gently asking, "What happened when Thor returned from Jotunheim?"

"There were some cliffs that overlooked the valley where Odin and his followers had moved to in the human realm. It was my favorite place and where Thor and I would often retreat to when we were tired of fighting with each other and just wanted to call a temporary truce.

"That was the first place we went when he came back. I'd like to think that there was still a small part of him that knew what he did was unforgivable."

Niall's fingers never faltered, and I focused on the consistent movement of his skin against mine.

"The bond between a valkyrie and another allows us to pull or push magic through the bond," I said in a soft, almost hushed tone. "It requires absolute trust because there is nothing stopping you from continuing to pull power even when the other has nothing left to give."

"Can't the other person stop you?"

"Yes." I turned my head so that I could stare at the painting across the room. Of a young valkyrie and Aesir agreeing to bond their souls together forever. "Unless someone has stabbed them through the heart and temporarily incapacitated them."

Those fingers never skipped a beat. Just continued to draw invisible patterns across my stomach.

"I lied before when I said valkyries always stab you in the front." Tears slipped down my cheeks, but I didn't bother to wipe them away, and Niall didn't comment. "I walked up to Thor that day and stabbed him in the back, piercing his heart with a poisoned blade. Then I held him against me as I drained his magic and his life."

"And this is why the valkyries treat you the way they do?" Niall gently turned my face back around so that I was looking at him once more.

"Our bonds are sacred," I said tonelessly. "I used the bond between us to kill Thor. That alone was bad enough, but I didn't die afterwards. I thought I would to be honest; it certainly felt like it. My entire soul burned, and I thought I would join Thor right there.

"But eventually the pain faded, and I discovered that his power now resided in me… and Mjölnir belonged to me. The fragment of his soul it contained should have left when he died, but for some reason it remained. I still hear his voice sometimes. See his face in others. I can never fully move on from him or what I did, because I'll always carry a piece of him with me."

The muscles along Niall's jaw flexed. "Why not get rid of it?" he asked, his voice carrying an edge.

"It's too powerful." I shook my head. "No one else can

wield it, but someone could potentially harness its power to fuel dark magic. That's why Gullveig wants it so bad."

"Can it be destroyed?"

Suddenly, the air in the room filled with static, and several loud crackle and pop sounds came from where Mjölnir still rested on the floor.

"Let's maybe not discuss that right now."

Niall grimaced but nodded. "Did your actions end the war?"

"Not entirely, but it definitely set Odin back and allowed my mother to lead a strike against him. She killed Odin less than a week after I…" I swallowed again. "A week after Thor died."

We lay there in silence for a few moments before I finally spoke. "Your turn."

The fingers stopped their tracing on my skin.

"Hey." I reached up and ran my fingers down Niall's jawline. "I'm happy to take whatever you have to offer, even if it's simply lying here with you."

He stared at me for a beat before swallowing and leaning down to kiss me again. I enjoyed the feel of his lips against mine before nestling against him and feeling him inhale a deep breath.

"A bargain is a bargain," he said softly. "I was young when I joined Balor's army, not even twenty years old. But there was nothing for me in the fae realms."

"Which one did you grow up in?" I asked curiously.

The fae realms were currently divided between the Seelie and Unseelie with the exception of Tír na mBeo that was shared between both courts.

"All of them," he chuckled with genuine amusement. "The sciatháin were nomads. We never settled in one place for too long and readily traveled between the fae realms. Things were different back then anyway; Unseelie and Seelie didn't exist. There were only the sidhe and everyone else."

"Well, that's still kind of true," I said with a heavy exhale. "Now the difference is that the Unseelie and Seelie are always fighting against the other while simultaneously turning up their noses at everyone else."

"Glad to hear some things never change." Niall picked up the end of one my braids, rolling the golden bead back and forth in his fingers. "The sciatháin weren't respected by the sidhe at all, but Balor saw our worth. Or at least, I thought he did back then. Now I think he was more like your Odin, good at seeing what drove other people and using that against them. The sciatháin wanted to feel needed, so Balor gave that to us."

"Did you have any family that joined with you?" I asked, feeling the need to be distracted against my own dark past and learn more about Niall. Even though I knew that like mine, his story wouldn't be a happy one.

"Younger brother," he said with a sad smile. "Back then, there was only the sidhe, as the divisions that made them Unseelie or Seelie didn't exist yet. But the beginnings of the break were there, and fights between the sidhe were common. When my brother and I were young, our family was caught in the crossfire of one of those fights. Our parents died, and I took on the responsibility of raising Thayer."

Given that Niall had walked away from Balor's army and had no interest in going back, I suspected that Thayer was no longer among the living.

My heart broke a little for Niall. I couldn't imagine taking on the task of raising a sibling only to lose them later in life.

My thoughts turned to Bryn and Finn. Actually, maybe I could. Even thinking about it caused me to start to panic, so I forced the idea from my head.

Niall continued, "Both of us idolized Balor, but Thayer did even more than me. When the fae learned how to travel between realms, Balor offered all of the sciatháin a place in his army. Almost everyone in mine and Thayer's generation signed up.

"The first couple realms we went to were mostly uninhabited. We'd stay for a few months exploring and creating maps of the area while Balor worked on opening a gateway to another realm."

"No fancy feline shifter to just snap open a gateway for you?" I mused.

"No," he laughed. "You lot are spoiled with Nemain and Badb."

"I'm guessing the fun realm exploration didn't continue?"

His expression fell then. "The realm exploration continued, but you're right in that it stopped being fun. Soon, some of the realms we visited had thriving civilizations… Maybe thriving is the wrong word, but they had people living there. Sometimes they were just as magically gifted as the fae, sometimes even more so, but more often less.

"Balor started trying to teach them different things. Some of the species we met were eager to learn, but some weren't for a variety of reasons…" he trailed off.

"I've never met Balor, but if he was anything like Odin, he didn't respond to criticism well." To be fair, I'd met very few fae who took criticism well, with Kaysea being an exception.

"I was never part of Balor's inner circle, so I wasn't privy to his private thoughts. At first, it seemed like Balor took everything in stride; sometimes we would stay in a realm for years, other times we would move on quickly within weeks.

"Everything changed when we arrived in a realm that had two powerful factions warring against each other because of limited resources. Balor listened to both sides, and whatever he heard made him respect both of them. The realm we had been to previously hadn't wanted any of Balor's help, and we had passed through it quickly. But it was sparsely populated… and had a lot of resources."

It was my turn to provide comfort, and I stroked Niall's wing before trailing my fingers down his side and massaging the muscles there.

I murmured, "Did Balor simply open a gateway for them? Or did you help wipe out the other civilization?"

Despite the harshness of my question, there was no judgement in my tone. My hands were stained with blood from Ragnarok, and I wouldn't be throwing stones anytime soon.

"That time, we simply opened the gateway before moving on." He shrugged with a casualness I knew he didn't feel given how tense his muscles were beneath my touch. "But that started to become a common occurrence, and soon when we reached realms that wanted nothing to do with Balor, he would order us to wipe them out so that the realm could be inhabited by others later.

"Sometimes, not always, some of the population would willingly join his army to save themselves from death."

"Those types of followers are never particularly loyal," I noted.

"Some of them deserted, or at least tried to," Niall agreed. "But despite how ruthless Balor was, there was something about him that drew people to his cause. He made sure that everyone who followed him felt wanted and respected. Despite all the fucked-up shit we'd seen, we continued to follow him.

"Thayer still loved Balor. I tried to raise my brother right… but it was always Balor he looked at as a father figure."

"I'm sure you did the best you could," I said gently.

"My best wasn't enough." He reached out to clasp my hand and studied our intertwined fingers. "We met strong resistance in one of the realms that resulted in full-on slaughter on both sides. I'm pretty sure that was the moment that Balor's sisters realized what a monster their brother had become and hatched their plan to trap him. Although, they likely also wanted to seize power over the fae realms.

"Even with Balor's absence from those realms, he was still the fae king." Niall's throat bobbed as he swallowed. "Thayer died during one of the skirmishes in that realm. It happened so fast, I couldn't even process it. He was there… and then he was gone."

"I'm sorry, Niall." I tucked myself into his chest, and he wrapped his arms around me protectively.

"Nothing really mattered after that. I just went through the motions as we tore through realm after realm until we became trapped by the fae queens. Balor started on his devourer experimentations, mostly using some of the soldiers who had joined us from other realms, the ones who were the least loyal. Most of those died, but once he started to perfect the technique, he asked for volunteers from the sciatháin, and I signed up immediately."

"You didn't expect to survive." It was a statement, not a question, and invoked a hollow pang in my chest.

"No," he said softly, "I didn't."

There was still so much we didn't know about each other. So many more painful memories and stories we might one day choose to share.

But we didn't have to work through it all at once, and there were plenty of other happy moments we could share with each other. And new moments we could make together.

I twisted in Niall's arms and brushed my lips against his. "I'm glad you survived."

His eyes darkened for a second, but then he pulled me to him and kissed me deeply before whispering, "Me, too."

Chapter Twelve

Hours later, I stood in front of the painting of me with Herja and Skuld. Sometimes, when I allowed myself to wallow in self-pity and grief for too long, I could admit that I missed them more than I missed him. Thor was my bonded, but they'd been my friends, practically sisters. The guilt over thinking such a thing always hit me afterwards. Niall came up behind me and wrapped his arms around my chest.

Once again, I enjoyed how easily he navigated around my wings, both in and out of bed. Heat started to pool between my legs, and my thoughts drifted to the things the two of us could get up to considering we both could fly.

Niall kissed my neck, letting out a satisfied sound as if he knew every dirty thought that had just run through my mind.

He murmured huskily, "I'm pretty sure we've more than outstayed our welcome here. We should find Badb and get out of here because I'm not sure if I'll be able to control myself if one more valkyrie sneers at you."

"Is that why you barely spoke while we walked through the town and in the throne room?" I ran my fingers through his dark hair that was looking rather messy and tousled. Which I decided I rather liked.

"I know your relationship with the valkyries is complicated, and I wasn't sure if you'd be okay with me ripping a few heads off." He tugged on one of my braids. "Personally, I think I should get credit for being so restrained."

"Duly noted and appreciated," I said dryly before turning back around to face the wall again. "I just wanted to look at this painting one more time because I doubt I'll ever see it again, and there's no way my mother will let me leave with it. She knows how much it means to me."

"They were your friends?" Niall guessed.

"Yes," I said softly. "We fought on different sides during Ragnarok, but we went out of our way to make sure we never battled each other. They fell towards the end."

My eyes reluctantly moved to the other painting, where Thor stood proudly in front of me.

He'd been so different then.

"Whenever you want to talk about it," Niall said, planting another gentle kiss on my neck, "I would love to hear about them."

I nodded, letting my gaze fall on the painting of the three of us one last time.

"Let's find Badb and get the hell out of here."

Niall followed me out of the room and down the hallway. My bedroom was towards the top of the tower, the levels above me holding the queen's chambers and the other throne room.

Part of me was surprised that my bedroom had been left alone and untouched. But then again, I'd never fully been able to understand why my mother did certain things.

It would have been faster to jump out of any of the open windows and fly down to the bottom of the tower, but that would have meant we'd have to interact with the guards outside the tower, and I had no desire to do so.

Instead, we made our way down the seemingly endless stairs until we reached the bottom.

The entrance hall was empty, and the doors to the throne room were closed. I halted and tried to think of where Badb could be. She might be further discussing the alliance with my mother. Or maybe she had returned to the village outside the walls to wait for us?

Before I could decide which option to pursue, Eylif strolled into the room, her standard haughty expression stamped on her features.

"They're upstairs in the war room," she said without preamble. "Collect the fae lover and get the fuck out."

She continued walking by us and out the tower doors. We watched her go, and then Niall slowly turned towards me. I immediately recognized the devilish look in his eyes.

"Don't," I warned.

"I just want to ask her to clarify who she means by 'fae lover'," he said innocently. "I mean technically, I think you and Badb both qualify now."

I scowled at him. "Just keep your thoughts to yourself for the next few minutes until we're out of here."

"What's in it for me if I do?"

"I don't bargain with fae." I narrowed my eyes at him.

A smirk spread across Niall's lips as he leaned in to whisper in my ear, "Perhaps not, but you definitely begged for my fae cock not that long ago."

"If you want to experience that again," I said lightly, "I suggest you behave."

He smiled. "Of course."

Voices filtered down the hallway when we exited the stairs on the second floor, and I slowed my pace.

The door to the war room was open, and they stood on opposing sides of the table, studying the map and documents spread across the surface.

"It will take some for the wards to be put in place," Badb said. "The magic is complex and requires both of the fae queens to work together. I think it makes sense to start with the realms that are at the most risk, leaving Vanaheim and Asgard for last."

"Fine," my mother snapped. "I'm sure that will make my daughter happy."

"I really don't understand your anger towards her." Badb paused for a moment, her eyes lifting from the table to scrutinize Róta. "We live complicated lives. The bonds we form not only help us survive them, but also make them something *worth* surviving for."

"Is this where you tell me that blood is stronger than anything?" Róta sneered. "That I should have cast aside my crown to help my daughter when she made that traitorous decision to turn herself into an abomination?"

I couldn't help but stiffen at the word. Abomination. That's all I was to the valkyries these days.

"That decision of hers brought Ragnarok to an end," Badb drawled. "It cost her everything. You should be fucking grateful."

My mother froze before raising her gaze to meet Badb's accusing stare. "If she had died afterward, I would have been. We would have raised monuments across all the realms, and I would have made sure to my dying breath that everyone only spoke my daughter's name with praise on their lips."

"You're angry at her for not dying?" Badb tilted her head and looked at my mother like she was trying to figure out what was standing in front of her. "What the fuck is wrong with you?"

"Sigrun failed in her duties. Both as a valkyrie and my daughter."

Only Niall's presence kept me rooted in place, otherwise I would have fled down the hall and let Badb find us later.

"I know about valkyrie bonds," Badb growled. "Her soul was intertwined with Thor's. Killing him was akin to killing herself and she *still* did it. Because it was the only way to stop him and save the valkyries, along with the rest of Yggdrasil. She sacrificed everything for you lot, and you fucking exiled her for it. She is your godsdamn *daughter*!"

"I would choose another daughter if I could." Róta's gaze never wavered from Badb's. It would have been less painful if she had slid a knife into my heart.

"Family is everything," Badb said. "Whether it be by blood or choice."

Róta scoffed, unmoved by the words, and returned her attention to the map before her.

Badb pondered the queen for a few moments.

"Once upon a time, I hated the fae with every fiber of my being. I dedicated my life to killing the fae queens." Badb's expression softened. "Then Kalen was sent to kill me, and everything changed. Both his life and mine. He defected from the Seelie Court and swore an oath to the Unseelie Queen. As did I."

"Is there a point to this besides love making both of you fools?" my mother mocked.

"We gave up our daughter to protect her from our long list of enemies." There was a slight crack to her voice as she spoke before she visibly steeled her spine and carried on. "Like me, she grew up hating the fae. She was fiercely independent and strong-willed, and it killed me to stay away from her as she suffered through life. One tragedy after another struck her and threatened to tear apart her soul."

I felt Niall go still behind me at Badb's words.

He'd only met Nemain once, and whatever idea he had made of her in his mind clearly didn't line up with what Badb described.

I'd met Nemain during those years when she was so angry and vicious after her parents had died. Even then, with all the tragedy following in her wake, she was still so wild and alive.

It was Myrna's death that had truly shattered her. In the years that followed, I'd feared for the first time that I might truly lose one of the only friends I had left. But I hadn't known how to help her because I was too broken myself.

"Her father and I had to stay away," Badb continued. "We had our own enemies to deal with. Enemies that would have been more than happy to target her to get to us."

The Valkyrie Queen finally lifted her head to look at Badb again.

"Despite our best efforts to keep her away from the fae queens and out of those dark and conniving courts, I watched her walk in with her head held high and join one willingly. Giving up her independence and forever altering her life, all so she could protect the future of a boy she barely knew."

Still, Róta said nothing, and I desperately wanted to know what she was thinking, but her face remained a mask of stone.

Badb bared her teeth, a feral glint lighting up her eyes. "She is my daughter by blood. *And* she is my daughter by choice. You were a fool to throw yours away."

"Your daughter is worthy." My mother shrugged. "Mine is not."

"*You* are not worthy of her. But that's fine. I have no need of another daughter, but I wouldn't mind having a sister to stand beside me once again."

Something in me stirred. A piece of my soul that had started to come alive when Nemain had introduced me to Bryn. And brightened further when Niall crashed into my life. Herja and Skuld had been like sisters to me. They were my equals who called me on my bullshit while supporting me all the while. The thought of having that again was like the final piece clicking into place.

Badb's eyes slide to the open doorway and down the hall to where I stood. "It's time you let go of the valkyrie. And became something else. Something *more*."

For a second, I thought I saw a flash of pain on my mother's face as her eyes fell on me and she realized I had heard every word she had said. But whatever I saw was gone in an instant.

Only the cold Valkyrie Queen remained, and she looked at me with distain before turning once again to Badb.

"It's time for you all to leave."

"Gladly," Badb said and strode towards us. "Kalen will come in my stead next time to continue discussing the alliance details. He's less likely to kill you than I am."

A gateway snapped open next to us, revealing the apartment Kalen and Badb shared in Emerald Bay. It still startled me how easily Badb could open these gateways; it took Nemain at least a few seconds of concentrating, but Badb opened them as easily as she breathed.

"Are you ready, valkyrie?"

I looked at my mother one last time.

"Yes," I said. "Let's go home."

Chapter Thirteen

As soon as the gateway snapped shut, I let out a long, even breath. Seeing my mother and the rest of the valkyries had been painful but oddly cathartic. It wasn't like ripping open old wounds, because the wounds had never healed. Instead, I'd just let them fester and rot for centuries.

Now, I felt like I could finally let them heal. They'd always be there, and I was sure I'd occasionally irritate them. Badb was right; I didn't belong with the valkyries any longer. But that didn't mean I didn't belong with anyone.

I had Bryn, who was already such an amazing and strong person in her own right. Then I had Nemain, Magos, and everyone that came with them.

I subtly glanced at Badb and Niall.

People could be your home as much as a place, and I had finally found mine.

"What's our next move?" Niall asked, drawing me out of my self-reflection. His eyes met mine and I saw nothing but unwavering support in them.

"We need to uphold our side of the agreement," I said. "Find and end Gullveig."

Badb made a noise of agreement and tossed her raven-feathered cloak onto the back of the couch before walking into the small kitchen off the living room. Niall and I hovered around the island while Badb threw things from the fridge onto its butcher block top.

I picked through the food, which was basically all different types of meats, before grabbing the cured salami.

Niall frowned at the selection of meat.

"Badb and Nemain are feline shifters," I told him. "You get used to eating a lot of meat around them. Although, Nemain has a little more variety since she operates a half-way house for vampires."

Badb snorted at that before reaching back into the fridge and grabbing a bowl of cut-up fruit and placing that in front of Niall.

"Kalen prefers vegetarian options over meat when given the option." She shrugged.

"Since Nemain is back, I'm assuming Pele is as well?" I asked.

Badb shoved a handful of smoked salmon into her mouth and closed her eyes as look of pure rapture came over her face. After a minute, she finally looked at me.

She blinked. "What?"

"Is Pele back?" I asked again with a bemused smile.

"Oh," she said around a mouthful of food. "Yes, but she's probably with Nemain. If Kalen's not back yet, they're likely still with the dragons."

"Pele promised to get me information on Gullveig in exchange for my time in the seraphim realm," I explained. "But Asmodeus might be able to help me if Pele's busy."

I didn't understand what exactly was going on with the dragons. Clearly, things hadn't exactly gone to plan in the dragon realm. But I needed to deal with Gullveig first before I could help Nemain and Pele. Gullveig was only going to increase her attacks on me, and it wouldn't be long before she started targeting others.

She had already expressed some interest in Bryn. The last thing my friends needed was my problems exacerbating theirs.

They wouldn't see it like that, but I would. Plus, Gullveig was the last piece of my old life that I needed to put to rest. I *needed* to finish this.

I eyed Niall as he methodically went through the fruit bowl, sampling each type of fruit. When he tried a piece of pineapple, he frowned and looked at the remaining pieces like they were a personal affront to him.

Badb followed my gaze and then we looked at each other, understanding passing between us.

"He can't stay here," Badb said immediately. "No offense. I'm temporarily halting my plans to slowly cut him apart piece by piece, but I don't trust him either. I don't care how good of a lay he was for you."

Niall's hand froze halfway to his mouth before he slowly lowered the strawberry back to the bowl.

"What exactly are we discussing?"

"I need to go to The Inferno. It's a local daemon bar that Pele operates," I explained. "Her second-in-command should have the information I need to find Gullveig. But you can't come."

He opened his mouth to argue, but I cut him off.

"Aside from the fact that both fae and daemons frequent the bar, and they might be able to pick up on your devourer nature, you physically won't be able to enter. Pele put some heavy-duty wards in place to prevent anyone with devourer magic from entering unless they've specifically been approved."

"And how does one get *specifically approved?*" He arched a dark eyebrow.

"Pretty sure the fucking you gave Sigrun will help with that," Badb said wryly.

I gave her a stern look, but that only made her smile.

"We'll figure that out later," I said. "I promise we'll figure things out with Nemain soon. But the negotiation to protect the Yggdrasil realms is dependent on me ending Gullveig. And now that I'm reasonably confident Badb won't hunt you down and hack off your head"—at this, Badb shrugged noncommittally—"I think we need to prioritize hacking off Gullveig's head. You can wait for me at my place."

Trepidation rippled through me at the idea of Niall seeing my cottage. He'd already seen me naked and had tasted and worshipped every inch of my body.

But for some reason, him not only seeing my home but being allowed to explore it without me there made me feel all kinds of vulnerable. I wasn't used to feeling that way, and I *really* didn't like it.

Still, he had to stay somewhere while I went to The Inferno, and my place made the most sense.

"I'm taking this with me." He clutched the bowl of fruit to his chest, and Badb rolled her eyes.

"Fine." A gateway opened behind us, revealing a flowery meadow and my cottage behind it. "While you go to The Inferno to speak with Asmodeus, I'll track down my wayward mate and see what he's done with your furry companions. Wait for me at the bar, and I'll bring them to you."

"Alright," I agreed and reached out to grab a piece of what appeared to be dried venison from the butcher block. "I hope for all our sakes that Kalen kept Viggo away from Jinx. He was in a piss poor mood when I left, and they don't mix well on the best of days."

Badb huffed. "Knowing my mate, he made sure they did meet, and then he sat back to enjoy the fireworks."

———

WHEN I STEPPED out of Badb and Kalen's apartment, I was surprised to find myself only a block away from The Inferno.

We were still in the supernatural part of town that kept all humans out with a simple keep-away spell. But Emerald Bay wasn't home to that many regular humans anymore.

Mortals were odd creatures. At one time they had all been well aware of the supernatural beings that roamed their lands. They even worshipped some of them as gods and feared others as monsters. Then their fear turned into hatred and they started burning anything with magic they could get their hands on before they stopped believing in magic entirely.

The fae and daemons made it clear to everyone who came to the human realm to not flaunt our otherness, mostly because they didn't want to deal with a bunch of panicking humans. But now we could almost walk around as our normal selves and the humans would find some way to rationalize it.

Elisa and Bryn had gone to some event called "Comic-Con" and everyone had complimented them on their amazing cosplays. Bryn's wings in particular had been a real hit.

Still, most mortals grew uneasy around areas of concentrated magic. And Emerald Bay had a very high population of magical beings these days.

The only humans who remained were ones with small magical gifts themselves. They felt more at home here, with us nonhumans, than they did around their own kind.

I nodded my head in greeting as I passed others on my way to the bar.

The presence of an exiled valkyrie had caused a bit of a stir when I first started coming here more often, but the locals were used to me now.

Unfortunately, so were the lokis, who seemed to take a perverse pleasure in annoying me.

Then again... they kind of took a perverse pleasure in *everything*.

"Sigrun!" a group of young and very drunk daemons screamed as soon as I stepped foot inside The Inferno.

A table full of what appeared to be water nymphs looked at the daemons and then at me. Something about the one with brunette hair, innocent brown eyes, and ridiculously large breasts seemed familiar to me.

Don't do it, I narrowed my eyes at them.

Their cupid bow mouth smirked at me, and then they raised their pint glass in the air.

"SIGRUN!" the table full of nymphs that definitely were not nymphs screamed. This only encouraged the daemons to cheer again, and soon the bar was full of drunkards chanting my name.

My stare connected with one of the daemons who was tending the bar. Asmodeus's turquoise eyes lit up with amusement, and they tilted their head towards the dark curtains that separated Pele's office from the rest of the bar.

Just as I took a step towards the office and the blessed silence it offered, the sinfully pretty nymph popped up in front of me.

"Are you leaving?" they asked in a breathy voice. "Won't you join us for a drink at our table? We'd love to enjoy the company of a strong and mighty valkyrie."

They sucked in their bottom lip as they looked up at me with eyes that somehow managed to be both innocent and devious at the same time.

"Sten," I sighed. "I don't have time for your bullshit right now."

They didn't bother changing their shape, but they immediately dropped the whole "sex kitten vibe" they had going on and just gave me an annoyed look.

"Damn it," they said. "You and Nemain always spoil my fun."

"Maybe because your idea of 'fun' usually comes at our expense?" I crossed my arms as I glared at the loki.

Delicate fingers scratched their lush brown hair. "You… ah… still annoyed about the other week then?"

"When you and your buddies kept annoying my apprentice until she started thrashing you around the bar and got herself banned for a week?" I leaned forward into their face. "Yeah, Sten. Still a little annoyed."

"We just wanted to play with the pretty vampire!" Sten blew out a puff of air, knocking away the strand of hair that had fallen in front of their face. "Your little valkyrie just needs to lighten up."

"The pretty vampire politely refused your advances."

Elisa was a little more adventurous than Bryn, but she was head over heels in love with my apprentice, and I knew she'd do nothing to jeopardize their relationship.

I knew how lokis worked. Sten wouldn't drop this. I needed to give them something else to focus on.

"There's more than one pretty vampire around here," I said slowly. "One who actually looks a lot like Elisa but doesn't come with an overprotective valkyrie girlfriend."

Sten pondered this for a moment. "Pretty boy." They snapped their fingers. "Misha!"

I mentally sent an apology towards Misha. But he was an adult with no attachments, and maybe he'd enjoy the attention of the lokis.

"I have business to attend to." I stepped around Sten and tossed over my shoulder, "But I'll suggest to Misha that he should come here more often if you back off from Elisa and Bryn."

"Deal!" Sten said cheerfully. "And tell him to bring the adorable shy one, too. I *adore* the shy ones."

"Sure thing." *Sorry, Damon,* I laughed under my breath as I brushed the curtain aside and stepped into Pele's office. Maybe the two young vampires would appreciate the break from babysitting the terror that was Isabeau.

As soon as the curtain closed, the raucous laughter and loud conversations became nothing more than muffled background noise.

Instead of sitting at the chairs arranged in front of Pele's dark wooden desk, I walked over to the large archway that took up a good portion of the back half of the office. The gateway was currently shut down so no one could enter or leave through it.

Travel between the realms was controlled by the fae and daemons… unless you happened to know two feline shifters who could open gateways on a whim.

Noise from the bar briefly filtered in as the curtain was once again swept aside.

"Need to go somewhere?" Asmodeus asked.

I peered over my shoulder and raised an eyebrow at them. "I don't know. Do I?"

A close-lipped smile flashed across their face. There and gone in a blink. Asmodeus purposely walked across the office and took a seat at Pele's desk.

Today they were dressed in their standard conservative business attire, which meant they weren't expecting Pele to be back anytime soon. Nemain had been the one to clue me in on Asmodeus wearing more… alluring clothing on the days they were planning on working closely with the future head of the Daemon Assembly.

Once she told me, it became easy to pick up on the small tells that revealed just how much in love Asmodeus was with Pele. What none of us could figure out was if Pele knew this and how she felt about it.

I had no interest in sticking my noise in their business. Unfortunately for them, almost everyone else in our social circle felt differently. Last I checked, there was a betting pool going on that even my young apprentice was involved in.

"You found something?" I quickly stepped to the desk and sat down in one of seats, leaning forward eagerly. "Can you point me to a realm?"

Asmodeus pulled out a map and stretched it out across the desk. "She's in Acleonia. There isn't much left of the realm, as devourers swept through it centuries ago."

They pointed to a valley that was nestled in-between two mountain ranges.

"Here, to be precise. I didn't want to risk traveling there to confirm on the off-chance she would detect my presence and move somewhere else. But Nemain or Badb should be able to open a gateway close to her location. According to my records, Nemain did a job there for Pele a decade ago."

I blinked in disbelief at the map and then at the daemon sitting before me. Asmodeus leaned back in the chair, looking quite pleased with themself.

"How?" I demanded. "Gullveig has been shielding herself from all types of tracking spells, and she's careful about who she does business with. How did you find her exact location?"

"To be fair, this is an educated guess on my part," they said. "But I'm quite confident that I'm right."

I waited for them to continue, still not quite believing that they'd found what I'd been searching for so easily for months in a matter of weeks.

"You mentioned that a huldra was part of the attack that took place at your cottage previously."

"It wasn't really an attack," I clarified. "Gullveig used the draugr to distract me while the huldra and dwarves just ransacked my place."

"Regardless." Asmodeus waved a dismissive hand. "The huldra was clearly working for Gullveig. Yes?"

I nodded, furrowing my brow.

"Huldras have a tendency to shed a lot of hair. Some of the strands they shed contain DNA. I went to your place while you were gone and collected those strands. Then I used the DNA that was present in some of them to craft a locating spell specific to that particular huldra."

That close-lipped smile spread across their face again, this time it lingered with a hint of smugness.

"There is no reason for the huldra to be in that particular realm, but that is where they went shortly after the event at your cottage, and they haven't left it since."

Despite it being an educated guess, I knew Asmodeus was right. The huldra rarely left the Yggradsil realms, and when they did, it was almost always to come to the human realm. But they didn't bother much these days because the huldra preferred temperate forests over cities, and there weren't many of those left in this realm that weren't tainted by humans.

Another thought crossed my mind, causing unease to slither through my veins. My fingers brushed against the back of my neck where a small, circular symbol was branded into my skin.

"This spell you used," I said slowly. "It differs from the locating spells that rely on blood?"

They nodded. "Those spells pull the magic that is contained in someone's blood and track that. Mine only cares about DNA."

Shit. Blocking blood magic was difficult; the daemons had the market cornered on creating counter spells, and they were expensive as hell.

After getting tracked down multiple times by young valkyries who wanted to make a name for themselves by bringing me down, I'd gotten a counter spell branded on my skin. It wasn't as powerful as the one Nemain had gotten centuries later, but it was good enough to keep most of the valkyries from tracking me down.

Most of those in the magical community wouldn't think to combine science with their craft. But it was unlikely that Asmodeus was the first daemon to do this.

I pursed my lips. Once the use of DNA became well-known in the daemon circles, other species would follow suit.

"How can it be blocked?" I gave Asmodeus a flat stare. "And how much will it cost me?"

A rare mischievous grin played across their lips, causing their turquoise eyes to light up even more against their dark mahogany skin.

"Consider this one on the house." They held their hand out, palm facing up, and a metal cylinder flew from one of the shelves to land in it. Brilliant orange flames sparked to life in their other hand, and they held the end of the seal over them.

I looked at Asmodeus with surprise and suspicion. They were being awfully cavalier about showing off their abilities. In all the time I had known them, I'd never once seen Asmodeus use their fire magic even though I knew they had it. I had no idea until now that they were also telekinetic.

Them revealing their abilities was a deliberate choice on their part; I just didn't understand why.

The flames receded into the stamp with a pop, and Asmodeus held their hand out to me. I looked at their extended hand and then met their gaze, holding it once more, a question in my eyes.

"A war is coming," they said quietly. "*Balor* is coming. I can see all the pieces he's moving around. The alliances he's form-ing. If we don't make alliances of our own, we will fail. There aren't many people I trust. I'm aware that you and I don't know each other that well. But I also know what you've done. The choice you had to make."

I went still at their words. While I wasn't surprised that Asmodeus knew that Thor had been my bond, and that I had been the one to end him, something in their tone told me that they fully understood what it had done to me.

Killing someone you loved was hard. It cleaved your soul in two and left you holding the pieces. But that was the *easy* part. It was learning to live with what you had done that felt impossible at times. I wondered who it was that Asmodeus had killed that had left such a mark on them.

"For that alone, I would *consider* trusting you," they continued. "The fact that Nemain, our sometimes paranoid, prone to violence, and almost never-trusting Nemain considers you a friend and an ally… That's enough for me. We need to trust each other in this."

The corners of my mouth quirked up into a grin. "She really does live and breathe violence. Maybe the kids are right that she needs therapy."

Asmodeus let out a light, almost delicate snort. "Pretty sure that's what her sessions with Pele are for."

Right. I'd almost forgotten that Nemain and Pele were a thing. Sort of. I didn't really understand how two people could be friends who occasionally slept together without it becoming more than that. But somehow, those two had been doing it for centuries.

I chewed on my bottom lip. If there ever was a time to ask and sate my curiosity, it would be now.

"That doesn't bother you?" I asked, and Asmodeus's dark brows rose in confusion. "That Pele and Nemain are…" I searched for the words that Kaysea liked to use. "Friends with benefits?"

They shook their head, amusement dancing across their face. "Polyamorous relationships are common amongst daemons."

"Huh." I placed my wrist into Asmodeus's still outstretched hand. "You guys are weird."

They raised a brow. "Valkyries bond their soul to another

and then literally die to awaken their powers. Also, you lot reproduce asexually by stealing bits of pieces from others. I'd wager your magic steals DNA in that process because valkyrie daughters are not exact copies of their mothers. And you think polyamory is weird? Might I warn you about stones in glass houses?"

They chuckled and pressed the stamp firmly into my wrist; it was warm to the touch but didn't burn. Magic tingled against my skin as they held it there.

After a moment, they raised the stamp, and I pulled my arm back. The faint markings of a DNA strand with a circle around it were imprinted into my skin. It still tingled, but I knew from experience that it would fade within a few minutes.

I met Asmodeus's stare once more and grinned. "It's taken me some time, but I'm beginning to realize that life's more fun when you're weird."

Chapter Fourteen

THANKFULLY, the lokis were gone when I exited Pele's office. Gods only knew what type of havoc they were creating around town, but that wasn't my problem.

"Sigrun!" a cheery voice called from the bar.

"Hello, Zareen," I greeted the daemon as I sat on one of the available stools.

"One sec!" She slid a pint of brown ale in front of me before scurrying through the double doors that led to the kitchen.

I huffed a laugh as I took a deep drink and enjoyed the smooth, almost nutty flavor. It was probably sacrilege for me to think the daemons brewed better ale than anyone in Yggradsil, but in for a penny…

The kitchen doors swung open, and Zareen practically pranced out.

I still found Zareen's fearsome appearance amusing considering her sunny personality.

While Pele and Asmodeus had this otherworldly beauty to them with their rich, red-toned skin and vibrant turquoise eyes.

Meanwhile, Zareen looked like something from your nightmares.

Her red skin was several shades lighter, and it contrasted sharply with her inky black hair and solid black eyes. The ram horns that spiraled out of her unruly curls only added to her demonic image.

I'd learned not to judge people based on their appearance, but even I had been slightly taken aback the first time I'd seen Zareen.

But Zareen's terrifying appearance fell apart as soon as she spoke and you realized that it was hard to find a kinder person than her. Or one who could bake such good pies.

"Pumpkin?" I asked hopefully as she placed a large piece of pie onto the bar.

"It is," she replied with a grin. "Kaysea requested it yesterday, and I managed to save you a piece before she devoured it."

"Can't say I blame her." I snatched up a fork and took a huge bite.

A moan slipped from my lips, drawing attention from a few locals who were also seated at the bar. Their eyes flicked down to the pie, and they snickered.

Anyone who came here often knew of Zareen and her magical desserts.

Zareen set about tending the bar while I scarfed down the pie. It didn't take me long. In less than a minute, I was looking forlornly at the empty plate.

"I'll make more soon, I promise." She planted her elbows on the bartop and studied me. "Haven't seen much of you lately."

"Been playing spy for Pele." I took another sip of ale with a shrug. "I'll be around more going forward. Just have one last thing to take care of."

Worried creases formed at the corners of her eyes. "Anything I can help with?"

I smiled at her. Despite looking like a hellish nightmare, Zareen wasn't much of a fighter. But between her employment with Pele and her growing relationship with Kaysea, she was very much a part of our circle.

"Honestly, that pie was just what I needed, and I didn't even know it," I said truthfully. "The last twenty-four hours have been… rough. I was overdue for something sweet. Thank you."

"Any time." Her eyes flicked over my shoulder, and I twisted on the stool to see Nemain stroll into the bar. "I'll be at the apartment tomorrow," Zareen said, and I turned back to face her. "I'll drop a pie off on the second floor so Bryn can keep it safe for you."

With that, she winked and moved further down the bar to check on the other patrons.

I huffed a laugh under my breath. The vampire brats lived on the first floor, and any food that entered their apartment vanished within seconds.

Food wasn't that much safer on Nemain's floor because that shifter inhaled food almost as quickly.

Zareen plopped down two more beers in front of me while chatting away with the daemons who had settled in next to me.

I grabbed the drinks, a brown ale for me and something that smelled super hoppy and bitter for Nemain, and headed to where the shifter was waiting for me at our usual table in the back corner of the tavern.

My pace slowed a little as I approached. She looked… tired.

"Oh, thank fuck." Nemain snatched the beer out of my hand and drank half of it down in a few gulps.

"Things went that badly in the dragon realm?" I arched an eyebrow as I took a seat across from her.

"Do things *ever* go well for us?" She shrugged and took another drink. "All things considered, it actually did go pretty well. We confirmed that some of the dragons are indeed working for Balor.

"Pele suspects that he's courting species that are powerful and have a chip on their shoulder to use against the fae queens. It makes sense; he only has so many warriors outside of his realm. But we still don't know what exactly he wants to do with them, so it's hard to plan for that."

"Maybe the information I collected in the seraphim realm will be helpful." My brows furrowed together. "The seraphim are also definitely working for Balor. Which means he's got dragons, seraphs, vampires, and warlocks. Not ideal." I grimaced.

Nemain smirked. "Well, we did take out a chunk of the bad dragons on our way out. Probably only put a dent in their numbers, but they'll be dealing with a power vacuum while they sort out leadership. Maybe they'll do us a favor and kill off a few more while they figure it out."

"I've never fought a dragon before. Could be fun," I said in a bemused tone.

"Have at it, my friend." She absently rubbed her forearms that were covered by the leather jacket she was sporting. "I've had my fill for a while."

"In that case, how do you feel about helping me hunt down a dark seidr practitioner?"

Nemain immediately perked up. "Pele found where Gullveig is hiding out?"

"Asmodeus actually, but yes, we have a location." I reached for my beer and wrapped my hand around the pint glass but didn't raise it.

Part of me was definitely eager to get this over and done with, but similar to how I felt after we left the valkyrie strong-hold, I recognized that this was another step towards putting my past behind me. The last step, really.

"Something on your mind?" Nemain picked up on the shift in my mood and tilted her head to study me.

Now that I had spent more time with Badb, it was impossible not to see the similarities between the mother and daughter. Although, I kept that observation to myself because I didn't think Nemain would appreciate it all that much.

"Do you regret it?" I asked softly. "The choice you made for Finn? Setting your life on a drastically different path?"

"No," Nemain responded immediately.

My eyes flicked up in surprise. I'd been expecting some hesitancy on her part.

"But you hate everything about the fae," I argued, my brows furrowing together in confusion. "The entire time I've known you, it's been you and Jinx against the world. Now you've settled down and live with like five million vampires, who you also didn't like I might add, and you serve the Unseelie Queen."

"First of all"—she pointed a finger aggressively at me—"I don't *serve* the Unseelie Queen. We… have an arrangement."

I gave her a flat look. As a subject of the Unseelie Court, she served Queen Elvinia. End of story.

Nemain turned up her nose, ignoring my pointed expression. "Second, I don't live with five million vampires, I live with six. And they're all house-trained."

"Last time I was at your apartment, there was tomato sauce and what I'm pretty sure was pineapple stuck to the ceiling."

She rolled her eyes. "Okay, they're mostly house-trained. My life is complicated." She shrugged. "Do I occasionally want to stab somebody? Sure. But that's what Mikhail's for."

I narrowed my eyes at the way her eyes darkened at Mikhail's name and the way she shifted slightly in her seat.

"Holy shit," I exclaimed. "You fucked him!"

"Fucking finally!" Zareen called out from the bar.

"Don't start," Nemain yelled at Zareen before narrowing

her gaze back on me. "I know where this is coming from. My mo—Badb caught me up on things."

I smirked. "Your mother is kind of terrifying."

"Not my mother," Nemain said automatically. "You've been dragging your past behind you like a boulder for centuries. It's time to move the fuck on."

"Duly noted," I said dryly, feeling a little better.

Nemain was right. And it's not like there was any going any back for me. The valkyries made it quite clear how they felt about me, even if some small part of me had been hoping that we could work things out.

But it was time to let that hope go and embrace the future I had right in front of me. "You want to grab your vampires and kill some shit?"

"You want to grab your fae lover and kill some shit?" Nemain gave me a sly grin.

"Badb needs to learn to keep her mouth shut," I growled.

Her grin widened. "Actually, she only told me that Niall was traveling with you. But I can smell him on your skin and took a guess."

"Fucking shifters." I raised my arm and took a sniff but didn't pick up on anything. Dropping my arm, I looked at Nemain. "Is that going to be a problem for you?"

"Why?" She slammed down the rest of her beer. "Because we tried to kill each other the last time we met? That's how you can describe most of my first encounters with people. Hell, you and I tried to kill each other several times if I remember correctly."

I snorted. She wasn't wrong. I was fairly certain that Nemain had never befriended anyone without threatening to kill them first. Even she and Kaysea had met under contentious circumstances, and Kaysea got along with everyone.

"Besides," she continued, "I let him live. It was Badb who

threatened to kill him if he came back, and she seems to be over that. So I'm good, if he's good."

"Thank you." I let out a sigh of relief.

Even though I suspected Nemain would be fine with how things were developing between me and Niall, it took a load off my shoulders hearing her say it.

"How serious are things between you two?" The playful gleam in her eyes was gone and now replaced with concern.

"Why?" I went still and studied my friend as she pursed her lips together in a hard line.

Her grim expression reminded me of how she used to be a few years ago, when she'd still be deep in her mourning of Myrna and hunting Sebastian. There was a trace of sorrow to it that sent a spike of fear straight my heart.

I narrowed my eyes and asked, "What is it, Nemain?"

"I'm not sure it's a good idea for Niall to come with us," she said slowly, a hesitant admission.

"You don't trust him?" I could understand why Nemain would feel that way, but I trusted Niall at this point, so she'd just have to deal with it.

I mean, she was sleeping with the former assassin for the Vampire Council, so she really couldn't throw stones here. Not only was Niall a good fighter, but I wanted him by my side. Something about his presence strengthened me, and I'd need that when squaring off against Gullveig.

"I don't trust him." Nemain shrugged "No offense. But that's not why."

She paused as she thought over her words.

More unease rippled through me. It was never a good sign when Nemain of all people was carefully thinking over what she was about to say.

"Out with it," I pushed.

She blew out a breath. "I shouldn't have won that fight."

Predatory green eyes met mine, and I knew immediately

she was referring to the fight between her and Niall. Each beat of my heart seemed to slow.

"The other fae had already roughed me up real good. I was poisoned and starting to lose control of my body. Niall is an amazing fighter. Adrenaline helped me rally a little bit, but he should have parried my strike."

The loud chatter around the bar faded away.

My lungs tightened around each breath, and I struggled to piece together a coherent thought.

She had to be wrong… had to have misunderstood what had happened. Nemain was a hell of a fighter. I'd seen her cut through dozens of warriors with her sword.

"You're wrong," I breathed.

"I'm not." She shook her head. "I thought about it a lot afterwards. Replayed the fight in my mind. I should have died that day. The poison had slowed me down, and I was barely conscious by the end. My strike against Niall was one of pure desperation. He was toying with me at that point, there was no reason he shouldn't have blocked that strike."

I bit back my denial. The fae didn't like to lie. Sometimes their magic did odd things with the words they spoke, and they were wary of unintentionally entering bargains. Nemain was part fae, but she'd never had that concern. I'd watched her lie her ass off on more than one occasion.

She did not, however, lie to her friends.

"I think that's why my ability to read souls kicked in; it picked up on what I was missing." Nemain held my gaze. "Niall wanted to die, and he saw me as a way to do it."

All those times I'd seen something dark and hollow in his eyes. This was what he'd been hiding from me. That easygoing persona he put on was fucking bullshit.

"Open the gateway," I said harshly. "Now, Nemain."

Whatever she saw in my eyes convinced her to comply with

my demand. She stretched out a hand and after a few seconds, a gateway opened revealing my cottage.

"I'll get Mikhail and Magos and whoever else wants to come and meet you in an hour or so. I should be able to pick up Gunnar and Viggo, too."

I was too pissed to say anything else. I just strode through the gateway and headed towards my home.

Niall owed me answers.

Chapter Fifteen

I STALKED towards the cottage and slammed the door open. My home was small, only consisting of a living space that had simple kitchen area tucked away in the corner, a bedroom, and a small bathroom that didn't even have a shower. I used the nearby river to wash up.

The living room was empty, and a quick check of the remaining rooms confirmed that Niall wasn't here.

My eyes snagged on the crumpled-up blankets on the chair closest to the fireplace. It was Viggo's preferred napping spot. I missed the cranky skogkatt and my loyal wolf. I couldn't even remember the last time we'd been apart for this long.

Nemain would bring them with her. We'd be reunited soon enough. I inhaled a deep breath, not letting go of my anger but letting it settle within me. Niall had some explaining to do, and he wouldn't get to dance around the truth this time.

The sound of metal striking wood came from outside. I headed out the front door and walked around back to where my workshop was set up.

Niall stood with one of my swords in his hands in front of a wooden practice dummy that was set up just outside the large double doors. His wings were hidden away, and he was shirt-less. Sweat clung to his skin as he admired the sword.

Lust and need surged up before the rage of what he'd been keeping from me smacked them right back down.

"Did you make this?" Niall raised the sword up, making the gold markings inlaid in the blade glint in the sunlight. "It's a thing of beauty. I originally thought it was too pretty to be functional, but the weight is perfect, and it slices through the wood easily."

"It's a technique I picked up from the dwarves." I closed the distance between us. "I'm not nearly as good at it as them, but I enjoy working a forge. It's become a hobby of mine."

Despite keeping my tone even and measured, Niall lowered the sword as he saw something in my expression.

"Sigrun?" He took a step towards me. "What's wron—"

My fist slammed into his jaw, and he dropped the sword as he spun around and crashed into the practice dummy. He recovered quickly and whirled around only to grunt as I sank a vicious punch into his stomach.

"Fuck," he ground out as he dropped to a knee and sucked in a breath, heaving for air.

"I spoke with Nemain," I seethed. "She told me a few more details of the fight you had with her."

Niall panted as he stared at the ground. Slowly, he rose to his feet, a wince flashing across his face as he forced himself to stand tall. He looked at me with his beautiful eyes and for once didn't hide the hollowness in them. The emptiness that he covered up with charming words and playful grins.

"You more than anyone must understand what it's like to endure for thousands of years when everything you've known and loved has been lost." The pain that coated his words threatened to break me. "I was tired, Sigrun."

Tired of living. The words left unsaid echoed between us.

"What exactly was your plan?" My voice vibrated with not

only rage but terror at the idea of losing him. "One last fuck before you rode into battle again? Can't stomach the idea of ending it yourself, so you want someone else to do it for you? I didn't take you for such a coward."

"That's not what this is!" he snarled before looking away from me. "I wasn't… I wasn't expecting *you*."

"That's not a good enough answer."

"Well, maybe I don't have a good fucking answer!" His head snapped back to me. He closed the distance between us until less than an inch separated our chests. "You know what it's like. The way we lose time. At first, the minutes slip into hours. Then days turn into weeks. Soon, entire years become a blur, and the next thing you know a century has passed but you don't remember any of it.

"And then you realize that you're simply going through the motions of living but you're not actually living."

My breath quickened at his words because I knew exactly what he meant. The thought of him dying was causing me to panic in a way I didn't know I was capable of anymore.

I might have found a new family that gave me a purpose in life, but I wanted more. *I wanted him.*

"Tell me what happened that day." I couldn't keep the tremor from my voice, but I had to hear it from him, even though I knew what he would say.

His eyes blazed, and black wings flared behind him as I tilted my head back slightly to hold his gaze, my own golden wings stretching wide.

"I'm no longer the boy I was when I followed Balor eons ago. My family and friends are long since dead, fallen in one battle or another. My people are echoes of their former selves, most of them so twisted by Balor and his experiments with devourer magic that they're not even sciatháin anymore."

His gaze bore into mine, and there was no force in existence that could have made me look away.

"What happened between me and Nemain… it wasn't planned. I really was trying to kill her. It wasn't personal, but it would have thrown a wrench into Lir's plans, and I cannot tell you how much I hate that prick."

"So, what happened?" I was curious about why he hated Balor's second-in-command so much, but I wanted to hear the rest of his story first.

"Nemain *is* really good," he said with a dry laugh. "Better than she has any right to be for anyone so young."

"Above everything else, Nemain is a predator. Killing is her nature." I liked my friend, and she had my loyalty. But I was well aware that Nemain lived and breathed violence and that she was a villain in a lot of people's stories. "On top of that, she's spent most of her four centuries of living honing her skills with the motivation that only comes to someone who has survived hell. Several times."

"I know." He swallowed. "Despite her skills, she'd been poisoned, and her body was weakening. I sensed what she was about to do a second before she did it." He swallowed. "I *chose* not to block it. When her sword slid into my chest, I didn't feel pain. Only relief."

His eyes searched mine for understanding, and I squeezed them shut before he saw.

Because I did understand. I felt betrayed and pissed off that he hadn't told me about feeling this way, but I also felt those things because I had felt that way myself.

I knew what it was like to ache for a release from the misery life often threw at you.

"After Nemain spared me, I didn't know what to do," he continued. "I thought I was going to die, was fucking happy about it. But then I was alive and being shoved through a gateway into what was basically a foreign realm to me. I don't know what to do, I don't know who I was anymore. It wasn't a lie when I told you I wanted to find Nemain."

"Were you hoping she would finish the job?" My voice rang hollow as I kept my eyes closed, fearing what his answer would be.

"Maybe," he admitted. "At first. I don't know. My mind was a fucking mess after everything happened."

"Do you still feel that way?" If he said yes, I had no idea what I would do. But I wouldn't let him go.

Strong hands gripped the sides of my face, and a second later, his forehead rested against mine. I let myself lean into him a little, breathing in his scent and feeling the warmth radiating from his body.

"Stay." The word tumbled out as panic gripped me. "Stay with *me*."

I felt him pull away, and I opened my eyes, searching his face for an answer, but his expression was once again unreadable.

My heart beat rapidly against my chest as I lowered my gaze. He was going to say no.

I was going to lose him after just finding him.

Niall tilted my chin up, forcing me to look at him once again as he brushed a thumb over my bottom lip.

"I'll stay," he said softly. "I am yours, valkyrie."

Hot tears ran down my face, and he kissed my cheeks, then my jawline, before finally claiming my mouth with his.

"I am yours, fae." I tilted my head back as he kissed my throat. "And if you leave me, I will fucking drag your soul out of whatever death realm claims you. You belong to me."

"Good." His lips trailed down my neck to my collarbone as he walked me backwards until my back hit the outer wall of the workshop.

Niall dropped to his knees and tugged my boots off before pulling my pants down. Instead of getting up, he gripped my ass and lifted me up.

"What are you—"

"Legs over my shoulders," he ordered.

Chills ran down my spine at the command in his voice, and I did as he said.

My wings flattened against the wall, helping with my balance as I swung my legs over his wide shoulders. Niall wrapped his arms around my legs and rose with one steady motion.

A gasp slipped from my lips as I steadied myself against the wall. I'd barely had time to adjust to the position when he licked his tongue straight up my slick, hot center before sucking hard on my clit.

I felt his warm breath against me as he laughed at the torrent of swear words that incoherently streamed out of me.

My core tightened as that wicked tongue of his swirled around my clit, applying just the right amount of pressure to tip me towards an orgasm without putting me over the edge.

I tightened my thighs warningly around his head when he continued his slow, torturous ministrations.

He tilted his head back and peered up at me with those deep blue eyes I didn't think I'd ever get tired of looking at and grinned. "Something you want?"

"I'll make you pay for this later," I warned.

"Guess I'll have to make you forgive me." His fingers dug harder into my flesh as he dove back between my thighs.

My back arched away from the wall, and it was only his firm grasp that kept me from falling. Quick pants slipped from my lips as Niall stroked me with his tongue, driving it over and over into my pussy.

Trembles racked my body as the pressure built and built. Just when I wasn't sure how much more I could take, Niall slid one hand down and circled my clit with one thumb as he pushed down on it.

A scream tore out of me as I came all over his face, and he continued licking and sucking me through it all.

"Fuck, I'll never get over how good you taste." He kissed the inside of my thighs, and I shivered before a single all-consuming need filled me.

"Put me down," I ordered in between panted breaths.

He did as I asked and smoothly set me back on my feet. I yanked him towards me, crushing my mouth against his, before spinning us around so that his back was against the wall.

"I can't be your sole reason for living," I said in a raspy but firm voice. "But I'm more than willing to be one of them, and to help you find others."

His eyes shone as we stared at each other before he dipped his head in a nod. "You will always be what brought me back from the darkness. But I'll find more in this new world."

"Damn right you will." This time, it was my turn to drop to my knees.

I didn't bother pulling off his boots, I just ripped his pants down and enjoyed sight of his cock springing free.

I tilted my head up and met Niall's burning gaze as I licked him from base to tip. He shuddered beneath me, a low growl rumbling from his chest.

"You're going to come down my throat." I swirled my tongue around his head, licking off the bead of moisture that had gathered there. "And then I'll give you a few minutes to recover before you fuck me against this wall. Hard enough that the fucking building rattles."

"As my valkyrie commands." The corners of his lips tilted up.

A string of curse words in a language long since forgotten streamed from him as I took him all the way inside my mouth. I felt both of his hands wrap around my braids as he bucked against me.

He didn't hold back as he thrusted over and over, and I loved the feeling of him sliding over my tongue.

With one hand on the base of his cock and the other on his

hips, I met his grueling pace. I moaned as a salty taste started to spread across my tongue, and my hand tightened its grip as he slid in and out.

He was large enough that tears were building in my eyes as he slammed into the back of my throat. I clenched my thighs together as a pressing ache started to build in my core even as I felt Niall tighten beneath me.

"Sigrun," he groaned before spilling down my throat. I greedily drank down every drop.

Once I'd wrung him dry, Niall pulled me to my feet and kissed me deeply. We both tasted like the other, and it gave me a heady feeling. I already felt him growing hard against me and silently praised the sciatháin for being blessed with impressive stamina.

His hands cupped my ass, and he picked me up and swung us around until I was pinned against the wall with my legs wrapped around his waist.

"Now,"—he slid inside me, and I gasped—"let's see how sturdy this building is."

Chapter Sixteen

Two pissed-off snarls sounded from outside the cottage followed by a loud crash. Niall instantly went on alert and rolled out of bed.

After the first round in the workshop, we'd retreated to the soft comfort of my bedroom. Well, technically we had round two against the outside wall of the cottage. But after that, we successfully made it to bed.

"Nemain's here." I let out a long-suffering sigh. "And she brought Jinx with her."

The front door to my cottage slammed open.

"Sigrun!" Nemain yelled. "Throw some clothes on and get your ass out here! Bring the fae asshole who stabbed me, too!"

"Come on," I said, rolling out of bed. "That actually was Nemain's version of being polite."

We quickly got dressed and headed outside to find Nemain, Magos, and Mikhail waiting for us beneath the large tree on the outskirts of my garden. Jinx had his glamour in place making him the size of a domestic house cat and was perched on Nemain's shoulder.

I looked at the two vampires. "Thank you both for coming. I realize this isn't your fight and—"

Magos cut me off, "We're your friends, Sigrun. Of course we will help you."

My throat bobbed as I tried to swallow past the knot in it. I jerked my head in a thankful nod, not trusting myself to speak.

"I'm always up for killing something," Mikhail chimed in. "Plus, if I don't keep an eye on Nemain, she'll get herself captured again."

A hiss tore out of Nemain, and her emerald-green eyes flashed in annoyance. "You got captured first! I let myself get captured to save your dumb ass!"

"Letting yourself get caught isn't a good plan, shifter!" Mikhail snapped.

"Well, next time I'll leave you to rot, vampire!" Nemain glared at him.

My eyes widened. "What *exactly* happened in the dragon realm?"

Nemain snorted. "We have a lot to catch you up on, and I imagine you have a lot to tell us about what you learned in the seraphim realm. Asmodeus and Pele are already pouring through that memory stone. Let's take care of your bullshit, and then we'll all catch up."

"Fair enough," I said and then gestured to where Niall was standing next to me. It didn't escape my attention that he had hidden his wings again. "Nemain, I believe you and Niall have already met. Niall, this is Magos and Mikhail."

I pointed to each of the vampires as I said their names. Magos nodded his head in greeting, but Mikhail offered the fae warrior a friendly smile.

Danger. Danger. Danger. The word repeatedly rapidly in my head.

"He's with me, Mikhail," I warned.

Those twilight eyes that seemed to always be promising

violence slowly turned towards me. "You had your fun with him. Now it's my turn."

Niall eyed the vampire. "You're very pretty, but I'm going to have to decline your offer."

Nemain chuckled, and Mikhail shot her a dirty look. "I'm still prettier than you."

She stopped laughing, and her hand slid towards a dagger on her thigh. The movement caused her long sleeve to ride up over the rise of her hip, and I blinked as I took in her bare forearms.

"Where are your bracers?" I asked.

Kaysea had gifted her the silver bracers shortly after Nemain moved to Emerald Bay, and I'd never seen her without them since.

Nemain flinched and Mikhail was instantly at her side, tucking a strand of her ash-blonde hair that gotten loose from her braid behind her ear.

That told me two things.

One, things really hadn't gone according to plan in the dragon realm. And two, things had changed between Nemain and Mikhail.

"They were a casualty of the dragon realm," Nemain said with a lightness that didn't reach her eyes. "Turns out even fae silver can melt under dragon fire."

Horror slammed into me as I understood what Nemain had likely gone through. My eyes snagged on the sword hilt peeking over her shoulder. Not twin swords, just one. I was pretty sure it was the one I'd gifted to her the first time she'd brought Bryn to visit me.

Apparently, she'd lost most of her favorite weapons. I hoped losing the swords wasn't as painful as how she lost the bracers.

I'd get the full story of what exactly had gone down in that damn realm once we took care of matters here.

Although, something told me Nemain wouldn't be forthcoming with some of the details. She had a tendency to hide her pain, even from those of us who loved her because she didn't want to burden others with her troubles. Stubborn fucking shifter.

Jinx leapt off Nemain's shoulder onto one of the low-hanging branches, drawing my attention to who we were missing.

"Where is Viggo?" I asked because one of those snarls I heard earlier had definitely been him. And if Viggo was here… "And Gunnar?"

"Bryn took them for a walk to cool off," Nemain said. "They won't be long."

I stiffened and shot her an incredulous look. *She didn't.* Even Nemain wouldn't be this reckless…

"Why is Bryn here?" I asked lightly.

Nemain cocked her head. "Why wouldn't she be here?"

"Damn it, Nemain!" I swore. "We're about to go up against the most powerful dark practitioner of seidr who has ever existed. Gullveig has bested almost every valkyrie who has gone up against her in the past."

"Good thing you're bringing more than just valkyries with you this time." Nemain shrugged a shoulder, clearly not concerned at all.

"Bryn is not coming," I growled and took a step towards her. "You will open a gateway and send her back."

"Will I?" The feline shifter studied her nails that had transformed to look more like claws. "Funny, that doesn't seem like something I would do."

"Nemain…" I took another step towards her, and Niall's hand shot out, latching onto my arm and holding me back.

"Perhaps we can discuss this and come to an understanding," he said smoothly.

Three sets of eyes widened as they took in the hand on my

arm that had halted me. Thankfully, Magos spoke before Nemain or Mikhail could make some smartass remark.

"Bryn understands the risks and wants to be a part of this," Magos said. "Like you, I was hesitant to allow her to come along, but she is an adult and a valkyrie. Her training has been coming along well, and she's powerful enough to not only watch out for herself but she's also far from being a hinderance in a fight.

"If you truly don't want her here, then we'll send her back, but keep in mind the message that you will be sending to her if you do so."

My lips flattened into a hard line as I inhaled a deep breath through my nose. Bryn would obey me if I commanded her to leave, but that would deal a hell of a blow to her confidence.

One of Bryn's greatest weaknesses was that she felt she always had something to prove, that she had to earn her place among us.

If I sent her away, Bryn would think I didn't believe she was capable of helping us in this fight, which wasn't how I felt at all. I just didn't want to see her get hurt.

But Magos was right. Bryn might be young, but she was a valkyrie, which made her damn near indestructible.

She could be hurt or contained, but killing her wouldn't be easy, and with all of us there in the fray, Gullveig wouldn't have the chance to work any truly dark magic against Bryn.

"Fine," I agreed reluctantly. "But one of us needs to keep an eye on her. If Gullveig gets the opportunity, she would abso-lutely try and kidnap Bryn while retreating. And we can't allow her to get away, especially not with someone who has as much magic as Bryn does."

"I'll watch over her," Magos promised.

She's coming back now, Jinx said from where he was hiding up in the tree. *Unfortunately, that sad excuse for a feline and the foul-smelling dog are still with her.*

"Play nice, Jinx," Nemain said firmly. Although, her words were undermined by the grin on her face and the wink she directed up to wherever Jinx was hiding.

"Are we all ready to go?" Bryn asked as she walked up to us, her always serious grey eyes landing on me.

My valkyrie apprentice had truly blossomed over the past six months. Once her valkyrie power had fully awakened, she'd put on another couple inches of height and a solid forty pounds of muscle. Her dark brown hair was now a dark red.

Despite her newfound power, she remained her kind and grounded self. Nothing seemed to shake Bryn.

Except Elisa and her ridiculous flirting. But Elisa provided an important balance to Bryn's stoic nature, and I was glad they had each other.

I cut a glance towards Niall, who was smiling at my apprentice. Maybe I'd finally found my balance too.

"Huh," Nemain said. "Not what I was expecting."

"It looks like your place," Bryn murmured.

She wasn't wrong. A small cottage sat in a meadow full of blue and pink flowers.

It didn't exactly look like the home of a dark practitioner of seidr, but I could feel the traces of Gullveig's magic all around us. This was definitely the right place.

"There are bones," Magos noted. "I can smell them."

Nemain wrinkled her nose. "That means draugr are likely in our future. Yay."

"Draugr aren't that much of a deterrent," I said. "She used nidling to track and attack me before, so I wouldn't be surprised if there are some lurking nearby."

"Draugr and nidlings," Mikhail drawled. "Plus whatever

fun creature crawls out of the lake. Maybe the kraken?" he asked almost hopefully.

He grunted as Nemain elbowed him hard.

"The kraken isn't here, and you're not fighting him anyway," she hissed. "He's a friend."

Mikhail's eyebrows shot up. "The kraken is real? And you've met it… him?"

A purely feline smirk played across Nemain's lips. "Jealous?"

Bryn sighed and gave me a long look. "Their flirting has only gotten worse since they got back from the dragon realm. It's also still really confusing."

Niall laughed softly, which drew Mikhail's attention.

I was pretty sure the vampire still wanted to kill the fae warrior despite Nemain telling him all was forgiven.

Apparently, Mikhail shared Kalen's opinion that Niall should still die. Luckily for me, and more importantly Niall, Nemain and Badb felt differently, which meant Niall was safe for now.

"The lake probably has nokken in it," I said. "As long as you stay away from it, they won't bother you. The nidlings are the biggest threat, but the draugr can't be discounted either. Their numbers could potentially overwhelm you, giving the nidling the perfect opportunity to strike."

"We'll handle it," Nemain said confidently. "Take out Gullveig and they'll all fall."

"Gonna use those fancy devourer powers of yours?" I taunted.

"Not unless I have to," she retorted with a grimace. "I might have taken on more than I could chew in the dragon realm, and I'm still brimming with the power I absorbed. I need a few more months at least to level out according to Kalen. In the meantime, it's difficult to control."

"Which means we get to play our favorite game." Mikhail

grinned, and a sword similar to Magos's materialized in his hand, mist rolling off it.

Surprise flickered through me.

Apparently, whatever had been blocking him from calling his sword was no longer a problem.

"What game?" Bryn asked, pulling her axe free.

"Who's the best killer," Nemain answered, a feral glint in her eyes.

I love this game, Jinx dropped his glamour, and the sleek hundred-pound black feline prowled towards the meadow.

You won't feel that way once I show you up, Viggo retorted and stalked after Jinx.

I glanced at Gunnar, and the wolf snorted before trailing after the two of them to make sure they didn't do anything truly stupid.

"Good luck," Nemain said before drawing the sword I'd made her not too long ago and jogging towards the meadow. Mikhail followed in her wake.

"Be safe." Magos nodded at both me and Niall.

The fae warrior stood by my side I watched my friends trip all of Gullveig's defenses.

The bones scattered throughout the meadow sprung to life, forming crude skeletons. The bones likely belonged to Asgardians and Vanir warriors, but the dark magic fueling them morphed them into humanoid monsters with dagger-like talons and jaws full of sharp teeth.

Six dark shapes came sprinting from behind the cottage. The nidlings had joined the party.

As much as I hated to leave my friends to this fight, Nemain was right. Once I killed Gullveig, all her dark creations would cease to exist.

Niall's steady gaze met mine as his dark wings furled out of his back, and the two of us shot into the air.

Chapter Seventeen

WE MADE it to the cottage unscathed, although I almost turned back at one point when I saw two of the nidlings zero in on Bryn where she was fighting some draugr on the ground.

But just as I started to change direction, Magos brutally sliced into one of them, nearly decapitating it.

That got their attention, and the nidlings quickly focused on him, allowing my apprentice to zip back into the air where she proceeded to dive bomb them.

Unless Nemain unleashed her devourer flames, they wouldn't be able to truly kill the nidlings or the draugr; all they could do was maim them. It was up to me and Niall to finish this.

There was no way Gullveig didn't know we were here, so I didn't bother with subtlety and kicked open the front door.

Niall guarded my back as we swept into the cottage. Unlike mine, hers was all one large open space, and it didn't take us long to see that she wasn't here.

My eyes raked over the room. Aside from the bed and dresser tucked away in the corner, most of the space was dedicated to spellcasting. A large cauldron sat in the middle of the room, and shelves lined the walls full of magical artifacts and supplies including a large jar of black scales.

"We'll need to destroy all this stuff before we leave," I sighed. "Anyone with an inkling for dark magic would have a field day here."

"Sigrun." I looked to where Niall was raising a trap door from the floor. "This entire room is dripping in magic, but it's even more intense down here."

I moved across the room and peered down the stairs that were hidden behind the door.

"Gullveig always did have a thing for caverns." I frowned into the dark that awaited us, really not loving the idea of being trapped underground, but we had no choice but to proceed.

"Let me go first," Niall said. "I'll have the best chance of seeing any magic heading our way, and even if I can't, my devourer magic should be able to absorb the worst of it."

"Fine," I reluctantly agreed.

Niall nimbly made his way down the stairs while I followed close behind. As soon as we reached the bottom, torches blazed to life with dark green flames, casting the narrow passageway in a ghoulish glow.

Yep. Gullveig was definitely expecting us.

Apprehension washed over me, and I pulled the hammer free from my back as I tucked my wings in tight. Niall's wings vanished once again, and he brandished his sword and dagger, clearly feeling as tense about this as I was.

"Come along now," Gullveig's voice echoed from everywhere and nowhere at once. "Don't keep me waiting."

Niall and I exchanged a pensive look before continuing down the passageway as it took us further underground before opening into a vast cave.

A tall, willowy figure awaited us in the middle. Black hair streaked with silver fell in long, tangled curls to her waist, and startling purple eyes took us in from an ageless face. A memory of an underground lake rippled in my mind. The last time I'd fought Gullveig in her true form and not through a body she had merely possessed. Back then, she'd summoned a tentacled beast that had dragged me into the murky depths and slipped away while I fought to get free.

I steeled myself. Whatever nightmares she brought with her wouldn't save her this time.

"Hello, Gullveig."

"Greetings, Sigrun." Her eyes flicked over my shoulder. "I see you brought your new fae pet along."

"Plus a few other friends."

"Ah, yes." Gullveig smiled. "My nidlings will enjoy the meal. Hopefully they leave enough of that sweet young valkyrie for me to use."

"You won't be getting your claws into Bryn." I spun the hammer around and took a step towards her when the entire cavern filled with a thick mist.

Within seconds, I lost track of Gullveig, and Niall was ripped away from me.

"Sigrun!" his growl echoed throughout the chamber.

"Niall!" I called back, but my voice was eaten up by the mist. My feet instinctively went in the direction where I'd seen him last, but I forced myself to stop and think.

I knew that Gullveig wouldn't come at me directly. In a straight one-on-one fight, I would destroy her in an instant. The only way I could help Niall was to survive the next few minutes and whatever Gullveig threw at me. Sooner or later, she would slip in her magic, and I needed to be ready to seize the opportunity.

A breeze flowed through the cavern, parting the mist. I readied my hammer, but a breath slipped out of me when a familiar red-haired valkyrie appeared.

"Bryn?" I looked at her in confusion but didn't lower my hammer. Something about her wasn't right.

The small smile she gave me was so much like my apprentice, as was the serious look in her eyes. Bryn always carried the world on her shoulders but never complained about it.

But this was not my Bryn. I was absolutely sure of that. What I didn't know was whether Gullveig had somehow possessed her or if this was an illusion.

"What are you playing at, Gullveig?" I growled.

"Playing?" the voice that poured out of not-Bryn's lips was so much like hers it gave me pause before I saw the axe head poking over her shoulder. Bryn's axe had been made by the dwarves and had a very specific magic signature to it. Despite all of Gullveig's skills, she couldn't replicate that.

"Stealing the faces of my friends isn't going to help you," I said coldly.

"Oh, I think it will." The fake Bryn ran her hands down her body. "This one is so young and innocent. I can't wait to take the real thing for a test drive later."

Magic from my hammer sparked, and those grey eyes latched onto it as a cruel grin spread across her face. Bryn had never grinned like that in her life, and it unnerved me seeing the expression on her face, even if I knew this wasn't truly her.

"How many young valkyries did you kill during Ragnarok?" she taunted. "How many of them were exactly like your young apprentice? Eagerly following the commands of their mentor?"

Deep cuts started to appear across this Bryn's body until blood coated every inch of her skin.

Bile spewed up my throat, and I swallowed it back down as the illusion changed. Red hair turned to brunette, then blonde.

Her pale skin darkened to a rich brown before switching to a tanned olive tone. Her grey eyes remained the same through it all, drinking in my revulsion at she easily switched from one valkyrie to another, over and over again.

"All that hatred you have for the seraphim," she tutted. "But they only killed a handful of your younglings. You cut down far more than that."

"It was war," I said through clenched teeth. "I tried to stop it."

"Did you?" The illusion's head snapped to the side as she once again took on the visage of my apprentice. "I suppose eventually you did stop it. But not before you shared your fair amount of valkyrie blood."

Blood coated my hammer and hands, and I watched it drip to the cavern floor with a numb-like detachment.

During the war, I hadn't been the one wielding this hammer. But the image of Thor returning from the battlefield with a triumphant smile on his face and the scent of valkyrie blood on his weapon was forever stamped in my mind.

A gurgling sound snapped my attention back to the Bryn illusion, and my breath quickened as coughs racked her body and blood so dark it was almost black leaked out of her eyes and mouth.

"Stop," I breathed, moving to catch the illusion as it fell.

It wasn't Bryn, the rational part of me understood that, but that didn't stop my heart from breaking as the valkyrie convulsed and died in my arms.

Hot tears tracked down my cheeks as I clutched her to me. My enraged screams echoed and bounced off the walls, as Gullveig's chilling laugh chased them. I didn't even notice when the valkyrie I'd been holding vanished and my hands dug into the hard earth.

"What's the matter, daughter?" A new illusion baring the face of the Valkyrie Queen taunted from where she stood above me. "Don't like the reminder of that lovely spell Odin crafted specifically to target unawakened valkyries?"

"He was a monster," I said numbly.

I'd always hated Thor's father. He was a trickster.

The lokis were tricksters too, but they weren't power-hungry. Odin only cared about power, and he would lie, cheat, and betray anyone to get it.

"And yet you fought by his side," my mother's voice said accusingly. "Would you have stopped me from killing him that day had you been there? Would you have chosen the Betrayer King over us?"

"What would you have had me do, Mother?" I half-snarled, raising to my feet so I could look her in the eye.

Some part of my mind whispered that this wasn't real, but it was drowned out by the rage and despair that coursed through me.

"Thor was my bonded. I loved and trusted him with every part of my soul. I never believed in the prophecy bullshit, but there were other reasons for fighting. So many of the Yggdrasil realms were unprotected and suffering, and you were doing nothing about it!"

Her lips curled. "Well, now most of those realms have perished, so I suppose it no longer matters." She gave me a mocking laugh. "Niflheim. Muspelheim. Jotunheim. Are they better off now? I suppose their souls finally found rest."

The hammer felt so heavy in my hand. I didn't know if I'd ever hated it more than I did in this moment. For everything it represented. Not just Thor and what had happened between us, but the destruction it had wrought at his hands. Even now, so many people wanted it and the power it held.

I didn't. I'd never wanted it. A piece of me wanted to drop it and walk away. Let Gullveig have the damn thing.

But you were always stronger than me, a masculine voice whispered chidingly in my head.

"What if I don't want to be?" I said softly.

"What's that, dear?" The Valkyrie Queen raised an eyebrow at me.

Magic sparked from the hammer and burned across my skin as if it sensed my thoughts and didn't like it. But no matter how I felt about it, the hammer was my responsibility.

I would never let it go, and definitely not to someone who would use it to inflict more pain on the world.

My fingers tightened around the handle, and the illusion that wore my mother's face only smiled as I pointed the hammer at her chest and pushed a bolt of magic out.

The illusion fractured as if it were panes of glass before vanishing in the air.

I sucked in a deep breath and let the hammer fall to my side as I tried to prepare myself for whatever Gullveig threw at me next. With every breath I took, I felt my resolve weaken a little.

The mist, I thought sluggishly. *She's doing something with the damn mist.*

I should leave. But Niall was still here somewhere. These illusions were well-crafted and had to take a hell of a lot of magic to fuel. Gullveig would only be able to do so many before she needed to change tactics. I just had to persevere and be ready to seize the opportunity to strike.

"Sigrun," a strong, deep voice said from behind me, and I momentarily forgot how to breathe.

"Not him." The words slipped from my lips as if they were a prayer. Joy and dread warred within me as I fought against turning around.

Heavy footsteps sounded as he took his time walking around to face me. I fixated on the dark animal hide boots that filled my vision until a hand gently touched my chin and forced my head up.

Brilliant blue eyes looked at me. They were full of confidence and strength with just a hint of mischief. The full mouth tugged upward into a smile.

"Hello, Sigrun."

"Thor," I said, my throat closing up at that one word.

His fingers slid across my jawline before brushing down the back of my ear and down my throat.

It wasn't him. This was just another fucked-up illusion, but gods I wanted it to be real. I was so tired of seeing echoes of his face everywhere. Of hearing the whispers in my head and never knowing if it was because of the piece of his soul contained in Mjölnir… or if I was just slowly losing my mind.

I wanted to remember our relationship that defied all explanations to outsiders. A love that could only be understood by fellow valkyries and their bonded.

A bond I had willingly destroyed.

As if reading my thoughts, he dropped his gaze to the hammer at my side. I fought against the urge to hand it over to him.

Not Thor, I reminded myself. But he was so real. And I was so tired.

"I see you still carry a piece of me with you," he said evenly, making no move to take the weapon from me. "I'm surprised you can bring yourself to carry it considering what you had to do to get it."

I flinched at his words, my eyes squeezing shut as my muscles trembled. Hot tears burned the back of my eyelids, and I fought to hold them back.

"You left me no choice." I struggled to get the words out. "That wasn't you at the end. The man I chose to share my soul with never would have done what you did." Slowly, I opened my eyes to meet his once more. "You slaughtered children, Thor. Innocent lives that were no threat to you."

"They were destined to grow up and defy me," he said smoothly. "What difference did it make if they died young versus old? You swore to always stand by my side. Instead, you stabbed me in the back and stole my power."

I shook my head violently, but he took a step forward, invading my space and forcing me to step back.

Another step. Another retreat.

My mind and my soul battled within me. One screaming that this wasn't real and the other just screaming.

The pain of our legacy was too much to bear, especially upon seeing him again. More of the mist swirled around; with every inhale, my mind became foggier.

"How could you do that to me?" Thor asked almost tenderly. "There is nothing I wouldn't have done for you. All you had to do was ask it of me."

No. The word slammed into my head.

This time, when the Thor before me took a step forward… I did not retreat.

"I did ask," I said harshly and took a step forward. He narrowed his eyes at me even as he took a step back. "I asked you to stop. *I fucking begged you.*"

Another step. The hammer was vibrating in my grasp as its power flowed through me. The fog lifted a little more.

"He was lost to me." I jammed the hammer against the illusion's chest and snarled. "YOU ARE NOT HIM!"

Lightning shot out of the hammer, striking him directly in the chest. His body seized up, but this time the illusion didn't fracture. Instead, it disintegrated into dust and fell to the ground.

I let more of the magic from the hammer loose. Bright bolts of lightning shot out, burning through the mist.

"Gullveig!" I screamed. "You're done fucking with my head!"

The smell of ozone filled the air as the mist burned away, revealing the bare cave walls once more. The rage coursing through my blood froze as I beheld what awaited me now.

Three Nialls were on their knees, each with their head pulled back and a shiny black blade digging into their throat. Gullveig stood behind each of them.

"Once again, the path you're on will require sacrifice," all three Gullveigs said at once. "Are you willing to pay it?"

Dark green flames flickered across the blades as each one dug a little deeper.

Two of the Nialls remained stoic, but one of them hissed in pain. Frantically I looked between the three, trying to find the one that was real. The Gullveigs all moved within unison, making it impossible to tell which one was really her and which two were the illusion.

"We both know that if you unleash the power of that hammer in here, you'll kill me." All three Gullveigs smiled. "But the drawback of that weapon has always been its lack of precision when used to its full potential. If you give into its pull and let it go free, you'll kill me… and him.

"Of course, you can direct it at one of us,"—they yanked on Niall's hair, exposing more of his neck—"in which case you'd better choose wisely because we'll slit this pretty fae's throat faster than you can try again. And trust me when I say that these blades will deal a mortal wound, even to a fae devourer freak."

Panic threatened to seize me, but I acknowledged it before shoving it aside. Niall needed me to keep my wits about me, which meant I needed to remain calm.

Electricity bit at my fingers, but I held the power of the hammer in check as I continued to survey each Niall, looking for clues as to which one was real.

"What's the matter, valkyrie? Having trouble deciding?" Her laughter filled the cavern. "I can see why you're hesitant to throw his life away. What with the bond trying to form and all. You may have survived severing it once, but I don't think you will again."

Time seemed to slow around me as her words sunk in. "Bond?" I asked, that one word cutting its way through my soul.

"You didn't know?" The three Gullveigs cocked their heads at me. "The beginnings of a bond are forming between you two. It's not quite at the acceptance stage, but it's close."

"That's not possible," I said flatly. This was another one of her tricks, it had to be. "Valkyries can only bond once in their life."

They shrugged. "That's what everyone believes because valkyries always die when their bonded dies. But you already defied that rule. Why not another?"

"Sigrun," the Niall on the far left choked out, only for the Gullveig holding him to dig their knife further into his neck, which caused the other two to do the same.

"Stop!" I said frantically.

"Put the hammer down and rescind your claim on it, and I will let him live."

"No." I shook my head. "Mjölnir has already been used to cause too much harm. I will not allow you to have it."

"That's my offer. The hammer for his life."

In unison, all three Gullveigs glanced up to the cavern ceiling before returning their penetrating gaze to me. "I'll even give your friends above the chance to retreat."

Mjölnir was a heavy weight in my hand. I couldn't give it to Gullveig. She was too powerful already.

Plus, it held a fragment of Thor's soul. It was only a small piece, more of an echo than anything, but it was still a part of him. He'd already been twisted into something dark in life, and I wouldn't allow this part of him to bring about more destruction.

Give me something, I pleaded as I looked at each of the Nialls. The one on the left who had called out to me earlier continued to struggle to get free.

The one in the middle attempted to fling himself on the blade to sacrifice himself, and I bit back a scream. The blade cut deeply into his flesh, and black veins started to spread out from it as he sagged on his haunches.

You promised you would stay! I wanted to scream before my attention snapped to the third Niall who was staring intently at me.

Niall promised to stay with me, to fight for a place in this world. And I believed him. He wouldn't go back on his word now, not even in an attempt to save me by giving his life.

He trusted me to figure this out.

"Time's up, valkyrie. We'll just have to see how well you fare after watching him die."

Just as the blades started to slide across flesh in one final cut, I snapped the hammer up at the Gullveig on the far right. The magic from the hammer obeyed my will instantly, a lightning bolt slamming into her and flinging her back against the cave wall.

The other two Gullveigs finished their cuts even as they screamed in pain.

Terror filled me as two Nialls fell to the ground convulsing, but that didn't stop me from running to the one I'd chosen to save.

I crashed to Niall's side just as a pissed-off scream sounded from across the cavern where Gullveig had landed. The remaining illusions froze in place before exploding into more sickly green mist.

"Good choice," Niall coughed as he clapped a hand over his throat, blood seeping through his fingers. No black veins spread from the wound though, so I took that as a good sign.

Gullveig rose several feet into the air, a rapid chant flowing from her lips as the mist started to swirl around us.

Niall's free hand slipped into mine. With my other hand, I raised the hammer into the air.

"Don't let go," I told him.

"I won't."

I looked inward, finding that new thread that was starting to bind our souls together, and a sob racked my chest.

The magic that linked me to the hammer flowed around this new bond, not only adding to its strength but marking it as a piece of me and therefore a piece of it.

Gullveig finished her chant, and the mist snapped into jagged pieces of glass that flung towards us. I didn't push magic from the hammer out; I simply stopped containing it.

The entire cave lit up in a web of lightning, burning through Gullveig and her magic plus anything else unfortunate enough to be here with us.

Niall held onto my hand as a thunderstorm that had been waiting centuries to be unleashed raged within the cavern. Finally, after what felt like hours, the magic faded, leaving behind one very charred corpse and nothing else.

Slowly, Niall and I climbed to our feet and made our way to the fallen dark magic practitioner.

The runes along my hammer were glowing, but I no longer felt the intense pull of the magic to be set free. I suspected the reprieve was only temporary, but maybe I could figure out a way to release it more often in the future.

I'd always thought of the hammer as Thor's. As the piece of him I was destined to always carry with me as punishment.

And maybe that's what it was at first.

But it was mine now, and I was ready to redefine what that meant.

"Is it finished?" Niall asked as he toed a piece of the corpse and it crumbled a little.

"Almost." With one smooth motion, I raised the hammer and brought it down.

Again. Smash. Again. Smash. On the final hit, one last shot

of magic bolted out, and the corpse exploded into fine powder before sinking into the ground.

"*Now* it's finished." I grinned at him.

"You just wanted to hit something with your hammer," he said accusingly.

"Just be glad it wasn't you for letting yourself get caught." I turned as we headed back towards the stairs that led out of the cavern. "Seriously, how exactly did an old and mighty fae warrior go down that easily?"

"Let's not talk about it." Niall grimaced. "Also, maybe we can not mention this to Nemain? She seems like the type to lord this over me."

I snorted. "Absolutely."

He glanced at me as we approached the stairs. "Absolutely, like, you won't tell her? Or absolutely, like, yes she will lord this over me?"

I went halfway up the stairs before twisting to look at him over my shoulder. "Absolutely."

Chapter Eighteen

"I ᴋɴᴏᴡ what Balor and Lir are planning," Pele announced as she swept into the meeting room on the second floor of The Inferno where she'd summoned us shortly after we'd returned.

She'd demanded that we come right away, but Nemain had flat out refused to go anywhere until she got the draugr parts out of her hair. Then Mikhail had joined her in the shower… so it took us a couple hours to get here.

Given the dirty look Pele was currently flashing Nemain and Mikhail, she knew exactly what had caused the delay.

"Oh goody," Nemain chirped.

Pele strode around the stone table that took up most of the room until she stood directly behind Nemain and wrapped her fingers around the shifter's braid before brutally yanking her head back.

"You're mine tomorrow night, and I will teach you the meaning of being kept waiting," she purred throatily into Nemain's face.

Well, I guess that answered the question of whether or not Nemain and Pele were still doing… whatever it was they were doing. Kaysea referred to it as friends with benefits.

As Asmodeus had already pointed out to me earlier, polyamorous relationships were fairly common amongst the daemons. It wasn't my cup of tea, but whatever worked for them.

I snuck a peek at Mikhail to see if he was bothered by this, but he was staring intently at where Pele was still gripping Nemain's braid. Nothing about his expression said he was upset by this. If anything, he seemed pleased.

As though he sensed my attention, his dark twilight eyes snapped to mine, and he winked.

Okay then.

Magos cleared his throat. "Apologies for the delay, Pele."

Pele rolled her eyes and released Nemain. "It's fine. Nemain never comes on time."

"Actually," Mikhail started, "she com—oof."

Nemain's elbow connected with his stomach, and the former assassin of the Vampire Council leaned forward, sucking in gulps of air.

Magos let out a bone-weary sigh, and I gave him a supportive smile. "You can always come and stay with me if you need a break from them."

"Please," Nemain snorted. "Like you and Niall are any better."

"We're not constantly stabbing each other!"

"I mean, he's stabbing you with something." Nemain smirked.

"I honestly cannot believe that everyone in this room is centuries older than us," a beautiful woman with fiery red hair said dryly from where she sat next to Eddie at the far end of the table.

She'd been introduced to me as Cerri and was apparently the reason Eddie had been so determined to go back to the dragon realm.

"I know," Eddie said gleefully. "Isn't it wonderful, my love? I actually seem mature in this crowd."

"Let's not get carried away," Kaysea scolded. "I'm definitely the mature one."

"Oh?" Mikhail arched an eyebrow at her. "Twenty minutes ago, you were recounting a story about you, Zareen, and several cans of whipped cream purely for the reason of making my uncle blush."

"That story made me blush," I muttered. Kaysea grinned.

"Anyway," Pele cut in, impatience stamped on her face, "I've gone through all the information Sigrun brought back from the seraphim realms, and given what we learned in the dragon realms… the news isn't great."

"Shocking," Nemain deadpanned.

Pele ignored her and looked to me. "Where's Niall? He's going to be a valuable source of information."

"He's resting at my place," I said. "He's more than happy to help, but the magic that Gullveig used on him is still wearing off, and he wasn't up for coming here."

I bit the inside of my lip, not really comfortable with sharing personal information about him, even amongst friends. "There is a lot in the human realm for him to adjust to."

"He's relatively new to the human realm, right? Up until recently, he's been locked away in the realm with the rest of Balor's army?" Cerri inquired, and I nodded. "Everything here is different. The human realm is chaotic. Even in towns like Emerald Bay where we barely interact with them, there is just so much here.

"There are a dozen different species downstairs right now. I don't know what any of them are, what they do, or what they want. And they're loud." She wrinkled her nose.

"Yes." My shoulders sagged in relief that someone here understood and that I didn't sense judgement from anyone.

"I'm sure he'll adjust with time," Pele amended. "In the

meantime, I'll come to your place tomorrow and speak with him there."

I smiled. "Thank you."

"So, what did you learn?" Nemain asked. "Why are there humans in the seraphim realm? How does that fit into everything?"

"There is one thing that the ward locking Balor and his army in their realm has in common with the protective wards surrounding the fae and daemon realms." Pele looked at each of us. "They both require magic generated by humans to keep them going."

"It's why the human realm is protected." Nemain frowned. "I don't know why it never occurred to me before, but that means there is a single point of failure for the wards. Take out the human realm, and Balor is free."

"Easier said than done. This realm is heavily defended by both the fae and daemons," Mikhail argued.

"True," Pele acknowledged. "But the fae queens have definitely thought about this. It's still a theory on my part, and we'll have to visit some realms to confirm, but I think they've settled humans in other realms as backup. In case something ever did happen to this one."

Nemain added, "That list of realms we found in the dragon realm. Some of the names had been crossed out."

"They're killing off the humans in those realms," I said. "Using species like the seraphim, who love to hunt humans, to do it."

"The seraphim probably bartered with Lir to bring some humans back to their realm," Nemain retorted in disgust.

"My father and his dragons would have been delighted to unleash themselves on an unsuspecting realm of humans." Cerri stared intently at the table, her eyebrows pushed together. "But if the fae queens set up these backup realms, surely they must know that they're falling?"

All eyes went to Nemain, and she raised her eyebrows.

"What? It's not like I'm bosom buddies with the queens. They don't whisper their secrets to me while we sit around braiding each other's hair. I haven't heard anything about this." Her lips twisted as anger brightened her eyes. "But I'll bet Kalen and Badb know and have kept this information from me."

A twinge of sadness hit me. If that was true, that would further strain the relationship that Nemain had with her parents, and I couldn't exactly blame her for being pissed. But after spending so much time with Badb… I knew how much she and Kalen loved their daughter.

"Maybe they don't know," I said. "Or there is something else at play here that we're not aware of."

"Maybe," Pele said, doubt clear in her voice. "We need to find out what the queens know. How many realms have fallen and exactly how many realms are needed to keep the wards intact. We've always assumed that only the original human realm was needed, but that may not be true."

Nemain's voice was light as she chimed, "On the plus side, maybe the prophecy around Finn is all bullshit. It seems like the realms are under threat for reasons completely unrelated to him and his magic."

I clenched my jaw as I recalled the fae prophecy. That the realms would fall unless Nemain somehow changed Finn's fate. Parts of that prophecy had already come to pass, with Bryn becoming a valkyrie and bonding herself to Finn.

He will bring chaos to the realms.

Gullveig's warning floated in my mind. I hadn't mentioned it to Nemain or Bryn yet and had no plans to.

It wouldn't change anything about their plans or their intentions towards protecting Finn. And I'd seen the damage that prophecies could bring when people tried to understand them or stop them from happening.

Never again would I allow a prophecy to dictate my actions.

"Balor and Lir are fighting on multiple fronts, and we need to do the same," I said firmly. "The seraphim must be stopped; they're too strong of a threat to be ignored. And we need to find out how to protect the remaining realms."

"I'll find answers in the fae realms." Nemain's eyes shone with resolve.

"We need to be prepared for retaliation," Mikhail warned. "Lir has likely been mostly leaving us alone all this time because he's been moving forward with this plot. Interfering will put us back in his crosshairs."

"Then we'll prepare for that too." I looked around the table, meeting the determined eyes of everyone seated. My friends. My family. "We'll make him regret ever messing with us."

———

When I slipped through the door of my cottage an hour later, I was greeted by a crackling fire and soft breathing punctuated by the occasional snore.

Viggo and Gunnar were curled up in front of the fireplace. I raised my eyebrow at Viggo, surprised he'd given up his favorite chair, but then I spotted Isabeau resting in it. No doubt she'd done it out of spite; she'd never fully forgiven the skogkatt for calling Finn an abomination despite the fact that he'd warmed up to the boy since then.

Everyone was worried about Finn and what he was capable of, but it was Isabeau who made me uneasy. She was part of our fucked-up family, and I'd defend her with my life. But what the vampire girl was already capable of and her explosive temper still concerned me.

My gaze drifted to the couch where Bryn was currently passed out on her side with her back against the cushions.

One wing was stretched out beneath her, and Finn slept on top of it, his back to her chest and her other wing draped over them both.

"Adorable, aren't they?" Elisa said, keeping her voice low.

She'd raided my cupboards, which were admittedly pretty bare, and had fixed herself a cup of tea.

"Yes." I quietly crossed the room to join her in the small kitchen area. "Would you be offended if I said I vastly preferred a sleeping Isabeau over an awake one?"

Elisa was the oldest of the vampire brats, as Nemain liked to call them, and happily took on the role of big sister. She was very protective of Isabeau.

I didn't know their full backstory, but I knew Elisa and the two boys had sacrificed a lot to keep the younger girl safe.

None of them were related by blood, but they called each other brother and sister regardless. The fact that they'd managed to escape the Vampire Council on their own was impressive and a testament to their devotion to each other.

"You're not the first person to say that." A wry grin spread across her face. "Misha and Damon literally begged me and Bryn to bring her here for the night with Finn. Got down on their knees and everything. I hope you don't mind?"

I laughed softly. "You're always welcome here. It's why I asked Pele and Asmodeus to lay the wards around my cottage and the surrounding area. Finn is just as safe here as he is at Nemain's apartment. Although, we might have to figure out how to build an additional story or something so that you all don't have to sleep in the living room."

"Pretty sure my brothers will be more than happy to help with that if it means they get more breaks from Isabeau." Her sharp gaze slid towards me. "They say thank you, by the way."

"For?" I raised an eyebrow.

Her grin turned positively devilish. Elisa was definitely spending too much time with the daemons.

"Sten and some of the other lokis basically propositioned them as soon as they stepped into The Inferno earlier today. That's why they requested to be off babysitting duty tonight. So they could *play*." She made air-quotes around "play" and then wrinkled her nose. "They're using our apartment, so gods only know what kind of mess they're going to make. I told them they have to sanitize everything before we get back."

I slapped a hand over my mouth as laughter poured out of me. Isabeau stirred slightly but then just pulled the blanket she had wrapped around her over her face.

"I was just trying to get Sten to leave Bryn alone. My poor apprentice can barely handle *your* teasing," I retorted.

"She's so adorable when she blushes, I can't help it," Elisa said, completely unrepentant.

"Of course you can't." I shook my head ruefully. My eyes darted to the closed door of my bedroom. "Is Niall sleeping as well?"

"He woke up a little while ago and went for a walk." Elisa's lovely blue eyes lifted from where she'd been admiring Bryn's golden wing and looked at me. "I like him. I think he'll fit in well with us."

"So do I." I smiled. "I'm going to go find him. A walk sounds nice."

"Of course. Enjoy your… walk." She waggled her eyebrows as the corner of her lips quirked up.

"Between the daemons, Nemain, and Eddie, everyone is a bad influence on you," I murmured as I strode to the door. "You need to spend more time with Magos."

Her quiet laughter followed after me as I slipped through the door and walked across the meadow to where the woods began.

Night had long since fallen, and I enjoyed strolling beneath the trees and listening to the various night creatures singing. There were large, winged beetles that thrived in this realm that went dormant for years at a time before they all awoke at once. This was one of the years they had stirred, and their low buzzing filled the night air. I found it soothing.

My feet carried me down a well-worn path. Before long, I reached a large tree that had wide limbs that stretched out almost parallel to the ground. Somehow, I knew that this was where he would go.

The muscles in my thighs tightened for a moment before I launched myself into the air, my wings flapping once before I settled onto a branch halfway up.

"Comfortable?"

Niall slowly opened his eyes from where he was resting with his back against the trunk and his dark wings wrapped around him like a cloak.

"This is an excellent tree for napping."

"I'm glad you like it." I smirked. "Because there are four people plus Viggo and Gunnar sleeping in my cottage right now."

"I noticed," he said dryly. "The small devil child woke me up when she shrieked 'pillow fight' at the top of her lungs and then Gunnar started howling."

"You get used to it."

"Do you?"

"No."

He let out a raspy laugh that sent a pleasant shudder down my spine.

My pulse quickened as Niall slid forward on the branch until we were mere inches apart. He traced a finger down my jawline before capturing my mouth with his.

When we pulled apart, I found myself breathless.

All from just a kiss.

His eyes glittered in the moonlight. "I did some exploring earlier before napping in this tree."

"Did you?" I tilted my head. "And what did you find?"

"Some hot springs. They're pretty well-hidden… almost seems like someone encouraged the vegetation to grow thicker in that area."

"If Nemain knew I had hot springs less than a mile from my cottage, I would never get any privacy." I made a face. "Despite being a feline, she will crawl into any pool of water and refuse to leave it."

"Well." Niall gave me a mischievous grin. "I promise to keep your secret, if you join me for a few hours in it."

I leaned forward and kissed him thoroughly before whispering across his lips, "Deal."

Together we slipped off the branch and walked through the woods, hand in hand. And I reveled in the peace I had finally found. That had finally found both of us.

Epilogue

LIR FOUGHT to keep the disdain off his face as the leader of the warlocks continued to doubt his plan.

Emir had been growing bolder lately. He was forgetting that all the power he and the other warlocks had amassed in the last few decades was only because he had allowed it.

Balor still believed the warlocks would play a vital role in freeing him and the rest of the army from that godsdamned realm. Lir had his doubts, but unlike the fool before him, he knew not to question his master.

His attention drifted to the seraphim guarding the door while Emir continued his seemingly endless list of complaints. She was tall and strongly built like most of them. He wondered how much fire ran in the seraphim warrior's blood and if she could call it forth.

In his time here, Lir had learned that for the most part, only the higher-ranking seraphs could wield blood magic.

But sometimes they would do something idiotic and get demoted.

Her light brown eyes flicked to his and their stares locked. Hmm... fire magic or not, he suspected she'd be fun to fuck later. The seraphim loved to fuck as much as they loved to fight, and they enjoyed both as rough as possible. This might be a backwater realm, but it certainly had its perks.

"Have you heard anything I said, Lir?" the warlock before him growled in frustration and the ancient fae warrior blinked, returning his focus to Emir once more.

"You've been saying the same thing for the last hour, Emir," he snapped, not bothering to hide his irritation at having his time wasted. "Nemain and the others need to be knocked off kilter. They already set back our plans in the dragon realm, and I've received reports about that valkyrie who runs around with them being seen in the seraphim realm. If they haven't already figured out what we're doing with the humans, then they will soon."

"They don't have the numbers to do anything about it," Emir argued. "We should be focusing on strengthening the warlocks and vampires. Once the fae and daemons start to actively get involved, they'll slaughter the lot of us. We *need* more power."

"And you'll get it. But without knowing how the sorcerers created the damn vampires in the first place or having access to the original devourer they used for the spell, it's not exactly easy to make improvements to their situation. I already have them yapping in my ear about still not being able to walk in the sun, and I don't need your voice there too."

Emir's mouth flattened into a hard line, but he didn't push any further. Good. He was a solid leader for the warlocks, and he kept them all in line. If he was forced to kill the warlock, then someone else would have to be found. Lir had better things to do.

"I'm surprised you were able to get the vampires on board with this plan," Emir said, his tone careful. "Nemain will rain down all kinds of wrath on them for doing this."

"They've been wanting to go after her for a while now. The

business with Magos and Mikhail, plus those vampire children who ran off a couple years ago, still angers the Council members." He shrugged. "I have no doubt that a lot of their numbers will be depleted, but I'm putting in a great deal of effort to figure out how to improve their magic. It's time for them to have more skin in the game."

"And if she wipes them all out?" Emir raised his hands defensively. "I'm not questioning your plan. Just trying to account for all possibilities."

"We have the seraphim," he retorted sharply. "They're arguably better soldiers than the vampires anyway."

Not nearly as smart, but he didn't say that out loud given that he'd set up his main base in their realm. The seraphim might not be the brightest, but they were quick to anger. He needed to make sure their rage stayed focused on Nemain and her allies.

"The dragons who allied with us are still recovering from the blow they were dealt in their realm and the loss of the leadership, but they're making progress," Emir said. "And I'm sure we can find others as needed."

"See that you do," he replied curtly. Emir wasn't wrong about the vampires being a potential sacrifice. Nemain was not one to be underestimated and he had no doubt she would carve her way through every realm to protect those she'd loved. In fact, he was counting on it.

Emir nodded and rose from where he'd been sitting across from his desk.

"Alright, I'll return to the human realm and continue helping the Vampire Council to make sure they have everything they need and check in with Artemis as well. The timing is going to be tricky; we have to snag them both in one go, otherwise the plan will fall apart."

"Do not fail in this." The words were a command as much as a warning.

"We will not," Emir assured him. "Preparations are underway. It'll take a few more months, but no longer than that."

"Good." Lir's lips curved up into a cruel smile. "It's time for Nemain to get a taste of just how much she's going to suffer for defying me."

Want to Read More?

The next book in the series, A Shift in Death comes out August 2024!
Signed paperbacks with character artwork are available on the
Greymalkin Press Shop at www.greymalkinpress.com.

Want to Read a Free Short Story?

Curious about how Nemain and Kaysea met? Want to read other short stories set within the Lost Legacies world? Sign-up for the newsletter at maddoxgreyauthor.com to get free short stories and stay informed of upcoming releases and events!

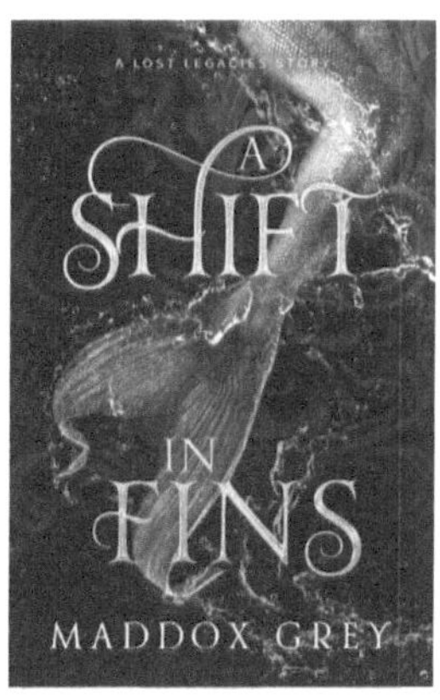

Acknowledgments

Thank you so much for reading A Shift in Wings! When I started writing Lost Legacies, I had a very specific plan in place. Seven books, all from Nemain's POV.

But then I had to cut a bunch of scenes from A Shift in Fate, ones where Sigrun was originally introduced. This led to me writing A Shift in Fortune, and I absolutely loved telling Elisa and Bryn's story.

It also gave me an opportunity to show Nemain from a different perspective and her changing relationship with Mikhail. And let some of the side characters get a little more page time.

So a seven book series became a twelve book series. With every other book being from a side character POV.

A Shift in Wings was challenging because Sigrun is so different from Nemain. My beloved shifter is a snarky, foul-mouthed rogue who is more than happy to stab people in the back and kick them when they're down. Sigrun is honorable with a dry wit. She's just looking for her place in the world.

When I originally wrote the scene with Nemain fighting the fae towards the end of A Shift in Fate, she killed them all and moved on. But something about it bothered me, so I rewrote it and that's how Niall was born. I didn't know exactly what his story was going to be, but I knew he was going to end up with Sigrun.

My mind is a weird place, and sometimes I just decide things on a whim like that.

I hope you enjoyed reading Sigrun and Niall's story.

They're not going anywhere, so we'll get to see them throughout the rest of the series. Whenever Niall isn't napping in trees, that is.

As always, it would be incredibly appreciated if you could leave an honest review on Goodreads or whichever platform you prefer. Reviews are super important for authors and we really appreciate it when y'all take the time to leave one! Plus, it helps other readers find us :)

Lost Legacies Guide

CHARACTERS:

Bryn - newbie valkyrie; her soul is bonded with Finn's and she is his guardian

Cerridwn - dragon, sweetheart of Eddie; daughter of the dragon who rules their realm

Cian - feline shifter with necromantic magic; twin brother of Nemain; has a strained relationship with her but still loves her fiercely

Damon - teenage vampire on the run from the Vampire Council

Dante - necromancer, incredibly powerful and in a long-term relationship with Nemain's brother Cian

Eddie - a dragon who owns and runs a shop of magical oddities and supplies

Elisa - oldest of the teenage vampire runaways

Emir - leader of the Warlock Circle

Finn - fae child of the exiled fae king Balor; a prophecy about him says he will bring about the end of the realms

Isabeau - child vampire that the teenage vampires take care of and treat as a younger sister

Jinx - a fae cat known as a grimalkin, him and Nemain have been together since she was born; he's grumpy and has the ability to inflict bad luck on others

Kaysea - mermaid princess and bestie of Nemain; Myrna was her twin sister; older brother Connor is very protective of her

Lir - fae devourer hybrid, serves as the right-hand of the exiled fae king, Balor

Luna - another grimalkin (because the only thing better than one cat is two cats); unlike Jinx she is sweet and cuddly

Magos - old vampire warrior, his past is a bit of a mystery but he's loyal to Nemain and their relationship is similar to that of a an uncle/niece despite not being related

Mikhail - former vampire assassin of the Vampire Council; nephew of Magos

Misha - part of the teenage vampire group, looks very similar to Elisa but they don't know for sure if they're actually related, either way they consider each other brother & sister

Nemain - feline shifter and fae hybrid with devourer magic; all around freak of nature; raised by Macha and Nevin who she only learned recently were actually her aunt and uncle; biological parents are Badb and Kalen

Niall - fae devourer hybrid who fought Nemain and lost, but she chose to spare his life

Pele - daemon who runs the local tavern, The Inferno; close friends with Nemain who she has been in an ongoing casual poly relationship with for centuries

Sigrun - valkyrie, exiled from her people after the events of Ragnarok; has a wolf companion named Gunnar and a magical cat named Viggo

REALMS:

*Note, this is not an extensive list of all the realms because there are many. Only those relevant to the story are mentioned.

Human Realm - the modern world that humans are familiar with; most humans are completely unaware that their realm is one of many or that magical beings walk amongst them
Meenri - the main realm controlled by the daemons after they fled their original home realm

Fae Realms

Mag Ildathach - belongs to the Seelie Court; name means multi-colored plains
Mag Mell - belongs to neither the Seelie or the Unseelie; like all death realms it is difficult to fully comprehend or travel in without necromantic magic; currently where Dante & Cian call home
Tír fo Thuinn - despite being referred to as a realm, this is actually a territory that stretches across all the fae realms, it is the dominion of the sea fae, all the oceans and seas belong to them
Tír na mBeo - only realm shared by the Unseelie & Seelie Queens

Fallen Realms

Kanima - former realm of the feline shifters; this is where Nemain's parents were born; it fell to devourers and the survivors fled to the human realm
Cerulle - former realm of Magos and Mikhail; also fell to devourers; survivors fled to the human realm and were later killed during the vampire and werewolf war

About the Author

After earning a degree in history and political science, Maddox was pulled kicking and screaming from the world of academia and thrust into the tech industry. Because they had bills to pay and nerd muscles to flex.

Whenever possible, they leave reality behind to build fantasy worlds filled with snarky morally grey characters and hot but devious love interests. Maddox currently resides in the northeast, but they'll always consider themselves Californian at heart. They live with their partner and faithful, but often stinky, furry companions.

To get regular email updates about new releases and other announcements, be sure to sign up for the newsletter on <u>maddoxgreyauthor.com</u>

facebook.com/maddoxgrey.author

instagram.com/maddoxgrey.author

tiktok.com/@greymalkinpress